Death by Revelation

K. M. Wood

Death by Revelation is a work of fiction. Any similarity
between characters depicted in it and persons living or dead
is purely coincidental.

Cover photo courtesy of the San Francisco History Center,
San Francisco Public Library

ISBN: 0615916392
ISBN 13: 9780615916392

Library of Congress Control Number: 2014909599
Sequoia Press, San Francisco, CA

For only in destroying I find ease…
Paradise Lost, Bk. IX

PART 1

Venice

Chapter 1

From where I sat parked in a red zone at the foot of Washington Boulevard, I could see the dark expanse of the Pacific Ocean and the white lines of foam where the surf curled and broke. A few feet away in the doorway of an untenanted store, a human form twitched violently under a blanket. When I turned off the engine, the downpour seemed to pound with new force on the car's corroding roof. Outside, the black, wet pavement gleamed with slithering ribbons of reflected light.

I had been to Venice, California when I was ten years old. I went with my mother to see an old friend of hers. My father, an alcoholic professor of English Romanticism, could not come along on that trip and stayed behind in Berkeley, and I still remember being surprised at how different life was away from him—how pleasant and safe it felt to be far away from his acid comments and boozy smell and general disgust with life. I was amazed at the change in my mother, who was quiet and colorless at home, but self-confident and animated away from him.

My parents' friends at home were all faculty, like my father. They were—so I thought—conceited people. I disliked them, and they ignored me. Maybe I was too young to appreciate them. But my mother's old friend, Enid, was different. She lived right on one of the canals and near the beach. A writer of screenplays for what used to be called B movies, she loved to tell her outlandish stories, and I now see that her amazing gift for telling must have helped her to market her work. Her friends and neighbors were also movie people: other writers, editors, and production types. There was a woman who dyed fabric for costumes and a fat young man who painted pictures that were used in sets.

Enid had a canoe that she kept tied to a little dock outside her bungalow. Every day, she took me out in it and let me paddle. She liked to cook, and she put nasturtiums in salads. I went to the beach and learned to bodysurf. I always seemed to have sand in my bathing suit and salt on my skin. Up north, this same ocean had a different identity—numbing cold with lethal riptides. Now, so many years later, acting on impulse, I was back in Venice to visit someone I hadn't seen for a long time.

Actually, I had come to LA as a favor to a friend, Professor Catherine Frankenstaad, who had directed my dissertation and for that year was Chair of the Renaissance Colloquium in San Marino. Suddenly and urgently, she needed a speaker to replace the scheduled and highly regarded authority on the tragedies of John Webster who had unexpectedly died. Catherine must have been desperate to have called on me, because I couldn't at that time any longer have called myself a Websterian.

I'd left teaching in the aftermath of my husband's death and had reverted to my old trade entered on in graduate school to provide needed income: formula romance writing. Until my marriage, I never had so much money before in my life, and there was also the fun of creating historical settings and pushing trite plots off of their centers.

Catherine did not approve of this vocation, and we had friendly arguments about it. But I wouldn't go back to the University. The associations were too painful: that was a different life.

But now she needed a Websterian, and I had an unpublished essay that was a close enough fit for her panel and that I could update. I was glad to be able to do something for her, and I had to admit that the idea of working on a serious project was intriguing. Predictably, as the day of my presentation approached, the whole business of preparation became rather pressing. I wanted, of course, to do a good job. I also wanted not to embarrass myself. These are both good goals. My publisher had left an excited message about some proofs of my current novel that needed attention, and I planned to call him back that evening. But he is a hypochondriac, and a conversation with him is always a commitment of at least forty-five minutes.

I had driven down to Venice to see my cousin, Katy. She had once been my closest friend, but I hadn't seen her in years, and that had seemed for the best, not that any definable break had taken place. We were the children of two brothers who had become parents in middle age, and as I sat there in the car with the rain coming down, I considered, not for the first time, the possibility that our friendship had merely been the consequence of being set against the grownups which, along with our shared sense of embattlement, adulthood had dispelled. Our conversations had grown strained, and it seemed as though, more and more, we disapproved of each other. After awhile, we just lost touch.

The truth was that Katy's mental problems made her difficult. She was gifted, but as a teenager, her mood swings could no longer be ignored and increasingly disturbed her comfortable and pleasant home. With her parents, my uncle and aunt, she visited psychotherapists, at last settling on a psychiatrist who prescribed anti-depressants and saw her through her high school and undergraduate years. She managed fairly well, as long as she took her medication.

Katy left graduate school after her Ph.D. exam and without taking the degree. She worked as a janitor for a San Francisco film director, became an apprentice editor, then an assistant editor, and so on, and eventually, she was working fairly steadily on feature films. But the long hours, pressure, and constant fear of failure were not healthy for her, and her work suffered. She was fired from a job, and then from another, and after that, no one wanted to hire her. She decided that she was finished in post-production, moved south to LA, and stopped returning my (infrequent) calls. The last I heard, she was working as a freelance story reader for a script agent. After my uncle died, I no longer had news of her.

I had made a serious mistake of judgment. I didn't have time this evening for a detour from my project. I'd spent the day in a UCLA Library cubicle reading up on lycanthropy. As the hours passed, the library cubicle had grown cold, and the aged Mazda, borrowed from friends, was unheated. I had on warm clothes—jeans, heavy wool sweater over a silk tee shirt, wool socks, and running shoes. But in the library, cold had seeped into my bones, and now I was going to get wet. I had a full evening's work still ahead of me, and I'd stupidly set myself up to pay this visit before I could get to work on my project.

I wouldn't call myself compulsive. In my current line of work, I'm productive without pushing myself unduly. But someone else's clock was running, and my Colloquium commitment hung over my head like an axe. My hand moved to the key in the ignition. Just go. Forget the whole thing.

There were other things that I wanted to forget, but that came back, sometimes, with all the cruel vividness of unwanted remembrance: what the doctor said—no treatment, not much time—and Alan's way of telling me with the usual kindness, more concerned with my feelings than with his own impending ordeal. Twenty-three days after the diagnosis, almost two years ago, he was dead.

I was teaching at the University. My friend Ed came back early from his sabbatical and took over my classes. I just stayed home. Even now, like the phantom limb, the neurological memory of a body part that no longer exists, Alan is there and not there.

Rainwater streamed over the car's windows. Everything outside was blurred.

After no communication for about three years, Katy sent me a postcard. In a way, I was pleased to hear from her. But I also felt the familiar uneasiness—and the shame that it always brought with it—at the possibility that I'd have to cope with her in a bad state and with feeling abandoned and resentful when she withdrew into herself, which could happen without warning at any time. Then, too, both of her parents were dead. My father was, let's say, not an attentive uncle. What would I have to do if she needed help?

So, I put off thinking about the postcard until, as I was packing for my flight to LA, feeling briefly but intensely alone, I felt an old pull and picked up the phone. My memories of Venice were another draw.

For October in Los Angeles, it was cold—56 degrees, according to the digital sign on a Santa Monica bank. The image formed in my mind of my audience at the Colloquium, polite academic men and women growing bored and even resentful, shifting in their seats, their patience sorely tried by my uninteresting, droning presentation. What I really wanted was dinner, a bath, a chance to call my publisher, a few hours of work, and bed. Instead, I faced not only a soaking, but also a reunion that I no longer wanted and that almost certainly would prove uncomfortable. Well, I thought, I could go back the way I had come and still salvage the evening. There was that option, but I wasn't going to exercise it.

I released the seat belt catch, opened the door, and stepped out into the rain. I opened my umbrella, locked the car, and breathed in beach air, for once, without enjoyment. This was not the Venice I remembered.

The nearest streetlight on Ocean Front Walk was out, so I walked in the dark and couldn't see clearly in the heavy rain. Some of the apartment buildings and houses were dark, too. Some had barred windows. On my left were the deserted beach and the rhythmic boom of the surf. Wind blew the rain under the umbrella and soaked my clothes. I had decided to head back to the car when I saw, just a few feet away, the address Katy had given me over the phone.

It was a low, U-shaped stucco 1920s vintage building with apartments facing each other across a narrow courtyard and a desolate little strip of sand running down the middle. An upright piece of rusted pipe in the center suggested an earlier time of fountains and high expectations. The apartments had French windows and glass paned front doors—amenities recalling a sunnier time. All of the windows but one were dark.

Katy lived in Number 2, and it was lit inside. Purple madras bedspreads served as curtains. I knocked, but no one came to answer. I knocked a second time, and still there was no response from inside. I turned the glass doorknob, and the door opened.

Time slipped away, and I was, or so it felt, in another world in which past and present fused dishearteningly in a small, humid, dimly lit studio apartment. It was the apartment of university days, but sadder because the tenant was not an undergraduate with all the promise of life ahead, but a middle-aged woman on a crash dive.

"Katy?"

I stood still for a moment and took in the depressing scene. There was the run-down building's characteristic odor of mildew mingled with leaking gas. There was a sagging couch upholstered in faded red brocade and a Murphy bed, clothes-strewn and unmade, with the bottom sheet pulled back at one corner of the bare mattress. The butt ends of two wires dangled from a disused ceiling fixture site. Someone had tried to patch the crumbling ceiling plaster with masking tape, but the tape had come loose, and brown strips of it dangled and drifted in the air currents. The only light came from an antique brass floor lamp with a decaying and torn silk shade that gave a yellow cast to the room.

When I saw the stained oak desk, I closed the door. This was the right place. Notebooks, pencils, some FedEx and manila envelopes were neatly arranged in a pile, and on top was a jar with something black in it. In this respect, Katy had not changed, for in her work, she had always been scrupulously organized. A portable typewriter occupied one corner. There was no computer.

At the center of this orderly tableau, positioned as though for emphasis, was an object which powerfully evoked the past. A big, very thick book with a loose front cover: *The Complete Dictionary of the Latin Language*, published in 1887, compiled by S.R. Anderson. That cover had been loose when I bought the book as a gift for Katy in a Clement Street bookshop years ago.

I'd meant it as a kind of gag. But seeing it there on that desk brought to mind one of the best things about our friendship. "Anderson" was a specialist's tool, and Katy had received it with a smile of real enjoyment. A good joke this was, to give such a thing to a modernist who had no use in the world for it, a gift from a Renaissance scholar to a student of an intellectually and artistically eroded period. Katy had understood this unspoken meaning and had taken no offense. She also understood that I saw myself as the less talented of us two, though she herself, as "Anderson" now eloquently reminded me, was generous and did not respect such comparisons.

I sat down at the desk. A key on a safety pin lay beside snapshots grouped in a heavily tarnished silver frame: Katy's father in tennis whites beside my father, his brother, in derelict fishing clothes, the sapphire waters of Lake Tahoe behind them and the purple mountains of Nevada against the sky; Katy's parents in front of their house on 30th Avenue with Pudgy and Duke, two beloved and obese beagles, like their master and mistress, now gone; Katy at the wheel of her Mercedes Benz two-seater. I remembered when we took that picture and several others, at least one of them with me in the driver's seat. I also remembered the time we drove to Calistoga for mud baths. Katy had run out of medication and was too busy with school to refill her prescription. She scarcely spoke to me during that whole weekend.

I looked around the room. Maybe it was pleasant during
the day with the sun shining in and people about—the place
was, after all, right on the beach. But that night, in the rain,
what a sad, messy, bad-smelling place, and it hurt to think of
my cousin living in it.

What had happened to Katy's movie earnings and the
inheritance from Uncle Edward? Mental illness is expensive,
especially if it keeps you from working. What about drugs?
Not likely. She didn't like the taste of alcoholic drinks, and
marijuana bored her. She never showed, at least around
me, the slightest interest in trying anything stronger. She
had her own way of coping with fear and unhappiness—ob-
sessive and usually quite brilliant work, her drug of choice.
How she'd found her way here was, I was sure, a long story,
some of which I would hear tonight, like it or not.

My watch said 6:10. I decided to wait another five minutes. The arrangement for this evening was between 5:30
and 6:00, depending on traffic. I hadn't called to confirm
when I got into town. But there was Anderson set out as a
welcome. There were the family pictures—I was in the right
place. Yet, I was beginning to feel vaguely uncomfortable. It
is usually better to let the past alone.

I took a folder from one of the neat piles on the desk
and opened it. The pages were typescript on old-fashioned
onionskin paper—where had she found it?—beginning with
the title, *Alfred Hitchcock: Artist of the Unconscious.* This looked
like the senior's thesis that Katy had planned to work into a

dissertation. It had seemed to me at the time so much better than anything I could have written.

I reached for the next folder in the pile. More onionskin continued the work.

What else was there? In a spiral notebook, handwritten pages of an immense annotated bibliography listed works on film, psychoanalysis, myth, cultural anthropology, Jung, Frazier, Campbell, Roheim, Ovid, the Grimm brothers, Bettelheim, Freud, Dante, Stekel, Sophocles, and so on, and on. Sources already consulted were identified, page numbers referenced, extensive notes taken on each work. She had consulted about a third of the works on her list. From the look of things, she was working her senior's thesis into a book.

This was familiar territory: Katy had numbered each page in the spiral notebook by hand. I found my San Francisco phone number scribbled on the inside of the front cover along with my LA phone number and the address of the Miller Place house in West Hollywood where I was staying. I remembered something else: how hard it was for Katy to finish anything. There was always one more source that had to be read, and one more edit. When the work was due, there was always torment and the gloom that came from the grim conviction that, whatever she had done, it wasn't good enough, ever.

The room was warm, and I unbuttoned my jacket.

One thick folder lay by itself. Inside on loose lined sheets, in typescript, was verse, a long poem that stretched out for about 50 pages. The title, *Cantos of Malediction,* turned out not to be inappropriate.

> Man-vermin! Child of slime! Earth scum!
> Dweller in feces, worshiper [sic] of garbage,
> Defiler, defiler, adorer of death.
> Bane of creation, Sathanas' whore:
> Malediction upon you, malediction perpetual!
> Oceans ubiquitous, lands to have deluged,
> In vain seek repose, howl for oblivion.
> Despair be your comfort, agony your pleasure,
> Orgasm of filth...

I put the pages down. Katy wrote *this*? Best not to bring it up.

The wall heater switched on, and, despite the near tropical warmth of the room, I began to notice that my feet were cold. A current of cold air was drifting across the floor. I didn't really need to turn around to know what I would see, but I turned anyway.

The kitchen was dark, but the edge of the back door was visible. At that moment, I was struck by my own stupidity, because risk is attached to an open door in a dark, run down area where people lie twitching in doorways.

I took a breath. At least now I understood the warm body-cold feet phenomenon. The heater was in the living-bedroom, and so was the thermostat, but it was directly in line with the open back door, so that the cold air from outside kept the heater going. I went into the kitchen to close and lock the door before leaving. I felt for, but did not find the light switch.

The inner side of the back door and the frayed curtain covering the glass pane were wet with rain. Had someone been here while I sat in the other room? Had Katy come in and left again, ambivalent as I was about our reunion and in a dark mood?

As I took hold of the wet doorknob, the perception of something odd in the room flickered at the edge of consciousness. A slow, fluttering movement of cloth—murky purple, like the curtain in the other room—and the electrifying perception of a skirt as the thing itself came into focus, crouching in that dark kitchen, backed against the refrigerator. Her hair covered her face, but I knew her.

Chapter 2

I had seen dead people before.

I was twelve years old when my mother died. Coming home from school, I knew what had happened as soon as I saw my uncle's car parked outside our house on a weekday. I went into her room on the warm September afternoon of her death and saw her wasted face and body still and lifeless, like a wax figure. When my husband died, I was with him. I was prepared for both of these deaths, as much as one can be. But I was not prepared for what I found that night in Katy's kitchen. The figure in the shadows was my cousin. Something held her to the door of the freezer compartment.

I don't know how I got myself out of there. I think I backed out, and I made it outside before vomiting. Then I headed for Washington Boulevard and called 911. I'd left my umbrella behind in the apartment. Heavy rain was still coming down.

I waited in the car for the police. Three men came out of a liquor store and stood in the doorway. They glanced at the man under the blanket, and one of them said something that made them all laugh. Now, the proximity of other human beings gave comfort. Anything was better than Katy's kitchen. I listened to the wind and the rain slapping against the car.

The police came, and so did the medical examiner, and I went back to Katy's apartment with them. I sat for a long time on the couch. There were wine rings in the layer of dust coating her coffee table. A woman officer was going through Katy's things. There was a large man in running shoes and a wet, rumpled raincoat. He had a receding hairline, acne scars, and a doleful but sympathetic face. The couch groaned when he sat down on it to ask me questions.

After awhile, Katy left on a gurney under a green plastic sheet. I watched the medical examiner's men push the gurney across the room and ease it down the front steps. Their shoes and the little wheels made scratching sounds on the wet, sand-strewn pavement outside.

I don't remember much that happened during that second visit to Katy's or later in the inspector's police station cubicle. I don't know how much time I spent there. I do remember that someone offered to drive me home, but I asked to be driven back to my car and drove with the windows open and the rain blowing in. I stopped once to vomit for the second time, opening the door and leaning out over the street. I shouldn't have been driving, because I was like a drunk.

The rain had flooded some of the storm drains, and on San Vicente, a large coral tree branch was down in the eastbound fast lane. It started to rain again as I turned from

Barrington eastbound onto Sunset. Visibility was poor, and water washed across the roadway like a tide. But I managed to get myself home, which, in this instance, was the borrowed house of a friend and her mother who were out of the country, a little hacienda type of place perched up above Sunset Boulevard on a narrow winding street, Miller Place.

The housekeeper had left lights on, and I closed the door on the storm. The contrast between this place and where I had been could not have been more extreme. In the comfortable, elegantly furnished living room, full of color and art, ambers and deep roses, I felt, reassuringly, the presence of my absent friends. This was real and Venice a hallucination.

Weak-legged, I held onto the banister going downstairs where the bedrooms were. I stripped off my wet clothes and brushed my teeth to get rid of the taste of vomit. I ran hot water in the long tub and undressed. A key on a safety pin was in my pocket. How had it come to be there? I could not remember. I do not fall apart anymore, I told myself. I will eat. If possible, I will sleep. I will go to the Renaissance Colloquium and fulfill my commitment.

The kitchen was large, bright, and designed for efficiency. There was a huge restaurant stove and a stainless steel refrigerator with a sub-zero freezer. Even now, refrigerators and kitchens remind me of that night and Katy as I had found her.

I drank some ginger ale and felt better, then tried grapefruit juice, and that also helped. In the freezer was frozen chicken soup, which I thawed out in the microwave and had with some egg noodles in it. I turned on the television on the butcher-block kitchen table and watched a PBS program about sharks while I ate. The rain stopped, and the vastness of Los Angeles spread out below, glittering with that brilliance that cloaks its banality at night.

There was no point in trying to work. I went to bed, and Sunset Boulevard carried out its night business down the hill—a smash-up, horns, brakes, yelling.

Opposite the bed, a small, wintry Pissarro oil hung on the wall. In the dark, I could see the general pallor of the scene. I tried to picture the details—trees without their leaves, a curving country road, a wall with snow banked up against it. There were small human figures in the middle distance. What else was there? I tried to concentrate on these things, and not on what pushed its way into consciousness at every opportunity: the crouching figure in the dark and my guilty, selfish self.

For years, the story that I told myself was, well, I could take or leave the relationship with Katy, and would probably leave it, never bothering to talk with her, my oldest friend, about our differences and our gradual alienation from each other. I had my own troubles, but even before Alan's illness, I had just turned away. Now I hated my self-absorption, my concern with projects and time management—as if it were possible, ever, for human beings to manage time—and my own cowardice. I sat up in bed and cried because I would never see her again.

But then I saw another way to look at what had happened. I switched on the night table lamp.

Katy and I had not been in contact for several years, except for a rather stiff phone call after Alan died. Then, she had sent the postcard, and we'd had a pleasant enough conversation and planned my visit. What occurred to me as I sat in bed was horrible. The invitation, the arranged meeting, the unlocked front door, even the back door ajar: all of these things suggested a most peculiar and ugly interpretation of events, that my cousin had planned her own death and orchestrated my visit so that I would be the one to find her. I actually entertained this insane idea for a moment.

I tried to focus on the quiet winter scene on the wall. It was like Celia's mother to hang such a valuable painting opposite her bed—exactly where she would enjoy it most—rather than in the living room to be exhibited to guests. The noise from Sunset had quieted. I switched off the light, and lay down again. There is a limit to what you can face at any one time, and just then, all I could try to manage was that my cousin was dead and had suffered badly, that I could have helped and didn't, and that I was now alone in a new way.

With the black outside turning gray, at last falling asleep, I remembered something I'd once read about the Middle Ages: that in those times, suicides were buried at crossroads. Having died in a state of sin, they were ineligible for burial in consecrated ground. Whatever suffering had led them, deprived of hope and in defiance of the teachings of their Church, to forfeit life and God, was to extend without termination after death. At the crossroads, the soul was to be suspended forever in a state of isolation, without mobility allowed—however much crossroads invite movement in one direction or another—with the configuration of the roads a grim parody of the Cross, symbol of mercy, up to a point.

Chapter 3

It was almost noon when I woke up. Outside, the storm had moved east leaving behind wild, unsettled weather and gleaming cumulus clouds riding over the mountains.

I cut the medical examiner's seal with Katy's key, unlocked the door, and went inside. The fresh and blustery day did not intrude upon the mingled odors of gas and mildew, and the atmosphere had the kind of density that I had felt in other rooms whose inhabitants had died in them. The curtains were drawn. I walked to the desk and turned on the lamp.

The room and its furnishings were the same as the night before, yet something was different: the place was clean. The dust that had drifted in clumps across the uncarpeted floor and the sand tracked in from outside were gone. The police or medical examiner must have cleaned the floor. I had the disturbing sensation of not being alone, but that, too, I had experienced in dead people's rooms. There was also the memory, overwhelming these reasonable assurances, of sitting in this very place the night before, not knowing that my dead cousin was in the kitchen, my friend transformed into a horror. Was she really gone? Or was she there even now, a lurking presence waiting for me in the shadows?

I walked to the kitchen and this time, found the switch and turned on the overhead light. The grimy surface of the refrigerator that had served as ballast in Katy's suicide now stood fully visible. The door leading outside was closed securely, but it was not locked. I worked the corroded bolt all the way into its housing. As though it mattered now.

Anderson was still in its place centered on the desk, a sad but affirmative message of welcome but perhaps, also, a malignant joke. Even in the light of day, I couldn't rid myself of this notion. I had brought along a small duffel bag, and I unzipped it and put the heavy book inside. For better or worse, the neatly stacked notebooks and FedEx mailers now also seemed to have been intended for me. I stuffed them into the duffel and zipped it closed.

Then I noticed that something was not as I remembered. One other object had anchored Katy to the past—the standing picture frame enclosing family faces—and it was gone. I looked around the room. It had been there last night…I was sure.

Someone had seen through the black tarnish and stolen the silver frame. Anyone could have come in through that unbolted back door last night. I switched off the floor lamp, went outside, and locked the door. The sky had clouded over again. Two tiny figures straddling surfboards bobbed on gray-green water beyond where the waves crested. I started to walk, but not in the direction of the car.

About a quarter of a mile or so to the north was a café. It had an outdoor patio surrounded by a low stucco wall and a magnificent magenta bougainvillea growing across the building and onto the tile roof. Over the door, "Café Bougainville" was spelled out in neon script. Inside I bought a latté from a large woman in a white caftan and turban and went outside to sit in the wind at a table close to the building.

Again, the old, abysmal feeling of abandonment. I had been through this before, death and loss. At least I had the notebooks. I pulled Katy's manuscript from the duffel, opened it, and confronted a prologue taken from Jung:

> There can be no question: the psychological dangers through which earlier generations were guided by the symbols and spiritual exercises of their mythological and religious inheritance, we today...must face alone...This is our problem as modern, "enlightened" individuals, for whom all gods and devils have been rationalized out of existence. [Campbell, p.104, cf. German]

This was not the comfort I had thought to find reading Katy's work. Was the irony intentional? Had she chosen the prologue material in a balanced moment? Or was this, rather, a poisoned intellectualizing about—and denial of—the illness which, in its gravest form, had released raw hate in *Cantos of Malediction?*

A man came out of the building, walking lightly and shielding a mug from the wind with his hand. He took a seat facing away from me at a table against the far wall. He hunched over his coffee, and the torn arm seam of his heavily soiled raincoat pulled open. A thin pony tail, greasy and sand-colored, lay like a starved animal on his back.

The wind rustled Katy's pages and scattered drops of water from the bougainvillea onto them, which I blotted with a paper napkin and read on and found my cousin again as I remembered her.

Clearly, despite her illness, Katy could still produce good work. This was not the masturbatory academic stuff churned out to get or keep a job. Whatever her state of mind, however advanced her illness, her work was carefully documented, intelligent, and original and written in a graceful and conversational style.

Sitting under the magenta canopy of the bougainvillea and gray of the sky, in a fresh ocean wind, maybe because of a latté that had gone straight to my brain, I had a wonderful idea. How Katy had felt about me, what I had done or not done, and the fact of her death were all inalterable. But I still had a chance to do something right, something positive, and maybe even soften my loss: I could finish her work and market it for her.

The man at the other end of the patio had shifted his ground and now faced in my direction. I went inside for a refill.

The large woman in white took my money. She wore four small gold rings in her nose and two studs in one of her eyebrows and moved with exaggerated slowness. Espresso making was not to be rushed. At last, she put the refilled mug on the counter, and I took it back outside to my table, which now was bare.

Disbelief. I stared.

Katy's manuscript—every page—was gone.

I'd left the duffel on it as a weight against the wind. The duffel was now on my chair. The man in the soiled raincoat had also disappeared.

A stranger took Katy's manuscript? What use could it possibly be to him—to anyone—but me? Why not take the duffel? It, at least, was useful. Was I imagining this?

I stood there, immobilized, tightness in my throat and a mean, angry stinging in my eyes. Then I rushed to the gate and for one instant, saw, or thought I saw, about a hundred yards away, something brown flitting between two buildings. It could have been anything—a paper bag blown by the wind, a dog or bird, anything at all, or it could have been the man from the café, clutching Katy's manuscript. Or maybe by now, he'd already thrown it away, or put it in his shirt to keep out the wind.

I grabbed the duffel and ran, skinned my hand on the gate, and headed south on Ocean Front Walk to the place where I thought I'd seen the fleck of brown. It was a narrow passageway between two buildings with a dogleg to the left, and I went in.

A Japanese elm in a side yard spread a canopy of branches overhead, and tiny yellow and brown leaves drifted in the air and onto the pavement. An old wooden chair had been overturned and blocked my way. Its cracked and peeling sea green paint was still glistening with rainwater, except for the underside of the seat, which was dry.

Every thought was focused on one overpowering need: to get that manuscript back. For some crimes you can be forgiven. But I would never be forgiven for this one. The only person who could have forgiven me was dead, and there was the strong possibility that for the rest of my life I would feel towards myself as I was now convinced she had felt about me at the end. I wanted that manuscript.

I reached the dogleg and rounded the corner. No one was there. I crossed to the other side of Speedway, went through another, wider easement, and stopped.

Here was a scene oddly familiar, insular, and domestic. Snug wood frame bungalows lined what seemed at first a narrow, shining, black avenue without cars. But this was a waterway, one of the canals dug out in the 1920's to realize a cigarette magnate's dream of reinventing the Italian Renaissance at a California beach.

The wind blew the surface of the black water into serpent scales. There were little docks, and on one of them, a mastiff was absorbed in licking his private parts. He and a few ducks cruising by were the only living things I saw in the gray light of that overcast afternoon.

Chapter 4

Through a fissure in dark clouds, sunlight shone with a peculiar intensity. It glinted off of the jewelry attached to the Café Bougainville counterwoman's face. The espresso cup resting in her big hand looked like a toy. A plate in her lap held a thick slice of chocolate cheesecake. Reclining on the cushion of an aluminum lounge chair, the woman faced the ocean and ate with absorption. The wind blew the caftan closely around the broad curves of her ample body, and her head, still in its turban, was tilted slightly back to catch the sun. She turned very slightly to watch me climb from the fire escape ladder onto the roof.

I have to admit that my appearance on that rooftop had a screwball quality, and I had a momentary urge to laugh. But the woman was not amused. I was intruding into a private moment with food.

What was to be said? I lost a manuscript, and I don't know how. A man in a filthy raincoat might have taken it, or he might not have. I'm a selfish and cowardly human being, and unless I get that manuscript back, I won't be able to live with myself.

"I'm sorry to bother you, but...Perhaps you remember me...I was here earlier."

Without reply, she returned to the chocolate cheesecake.

She was a beautiful woman with a lovely face and a flawless, glowing rose and cream complexion, but her expression was sullen.

Unmannerly, not asking consent, I sat down near her on an overturned milk crate. "It was about an hour ago, and I was at a table outside," I explained as she continued to eat. "A man was there, as well."

With a sigh, she ate the last bite of cake, and her entire being seemed silently to revel in that act. With a visible effort, she reached down for the espresso cup which she'd placed beside her chair on the tar and gravel roof surface. She sipped the hot drink and looked me over, an interloper wanting something. It was cold on the unsheltered roof.

"I lost some things when I was here awhile ago." It occurred to me that I hadn't tipped her. Perhaps that was the problem.

"I had some papers. That man and I were the only customers out on the patio. It was about an hour ago. He had a pony tail." This last detail I added, as it seemed, rather lamely. Better not to mention the coat, which to describe would seem a disparagement.

"I went inside for a refill, and when I got back to my table, the papers were gone. The man was also gone. I came back to ask if you knew him."

K. M. WOOD

The woman's sullen expression gave way to smirk of contempt that made my visit seem pointless.

"Those papers—they were a manuscript. It belonged to a
friend. She was a close friend, and last night she died."

The woman blinked: now this was interesting.

"My friend was writing a book."

"I'm sorry," the woman said. She spoke rather mechanically, but watched me attentively.

"I want to finish the book for her and have it published. I
want to find the man who was here earlier. He may have seen
what happened."

She emptied the dregs of espresso onto the roof and
heaved herself up into a sitting position.

"Do you know the man I'm talking about?"

"He's a street bum."

"You know him?"

"He comes in all the time. We give him stuff."

"Do you know his name?"

The woman got to her feet. The dessert plate gleamed,
immaculate.

I pulled a fifty-dollar bill from my jeans.

"What's that for?" She regarded the bill with distaste.

"I don't want to get anyone into trouble. This isn't a police matter. It's just a manuscript—of no value to anyone but
me. I'm not saying he *took* it. It's just that he may know what
happened to it. I've looked through all the trash cans around
the café, and they let me look through the ones inside. Do
you know where he lives?"

She shook her head, and I had the feeling that she found the question insulting.

Still holding the fifty-dollar bill, I said, "The next time he comes in, would you tell him I'm offering a reward? $250—each—when I get the manuscript back."

"I don't talk to him."

"I mean, when he comes in for food."

"I don't talk to him," she repeated. "And you know something?" She looked pointedly at me. "You don't want to find him."

"I have to."

"No, you don't." She turned to leave.

"Just tell me his name."

"Stuart," she said without looking at me.

"Stuart is his first or last name?"

"First."

"Stuart what? Do you know?"

With surprising agility for someone of her weight, she stepped onto the fire escape ladder and went down.

Up from the ocean, and old man and woman came hand in hand. They had been swimming in the cold surf. Dripping and, undoubtedly, shivering, they came across the beach and as they drew closer, I could see their deeply tanned skin like leather. Seeming to pass under the building on whose roof I stood and to descend into the earth, they disappeared and at that moment, I caught my breath. I saw what I had missed and what should have been obvious all along.

Notes. There must be notes. Of course. In any writing project, they come first. And, being a kind of safety net, they survive in a drawer or somewhere long after they are needed. It was certain that Katy, who fussed obsessively over every project, would have produced copious notes, and these, I knew, she would have been incapable of throwing away.

Chapter 5

I had never been to Katy's place on Ocean Front Walk before yesterday. Now, within 24 hours, I'd visited it three times, which was the pattern of recurrent events in fairy tales.

The rays of the sun slanted under the cloud mass and turned the ocean at the horizon silver. An old lady was sweeping steps of Number 2. They were clean, but she shook her head at them and straightened her black wig. Then she noticed me and said, "It alvays comes beck."

She was standing at the bottom of Katy's steps, blocking my way, and she looked hard at me with small, glittering eyes in a powdered face. Age had thinned her lips almost out of existence.

She smiled. "A death," she said and leaned towards me over the broom handle, gesturing with her chin towards Katy's window. Her eyes narrowed, and she calculated the effect of her announcement. "My daughter's tenant *hanged* herself."

The wind sent eddies of sand whirling across the pavement towards the newly swept steps. The old lady watched them with dislike. Noticing the key in my hand and with a knowing smile, she asked, "A relation?"

She could see that I wanted to go in, but she did not move aside. I waited for her to point to the police tape, still flapping in the wind, and to tell me I could not under any circumstances go in. I imagined *her* going in, as she must have done, to have a look around, especially in the kitchen. Now she was to enjoy the thought of someone else going in, knowing what had happened there.

"I told my son-in-law. There's something the matter in 2. Lights alvays on. Day and night. Vater all the time running. All the time. That's in the rent! How much vater does she need, a single person?"

I stepped around her and went inside, as before, enveloped by the gas and mildew smell. I sat at the desk, reached under the rotting shade, and switched on the lamp. Yes, I remembered the washing. It started in graduate school, and certainly graduate school could cause chronic disorders in anyone. I myself had suffered from headaches, stomach pain, and rashes. But these ailments were more or less common and manageable. I guess you had to have a screw loose to bother with graduate school in the first place. But Katy's problem had been of a different kind.

One of my earliest recollections from childhood is of Katy asking me why I touched things in public places. She would never touch railings or even pick up objects from displays in stores to look at them. She never had to be told to wash before a meal.

At some point early in graduate school, she read somewhere that soap was harmful to the skin. She would explain that it caused dryness, irritation, lesions, and eventually, infection. She gave up soap for a while and began to smell. Unwillingly, she began using it again, though she tried to minimize its destructive effects by careful and prolonged rinsing. Her skin became chronically dry, blotchy, and cracked.

I took time off from school after taking the Master's Comprehensive and went to Italy. When I came back about a year later, I stayed with Katy for a few weeks. She washed often—whenever she got up from her desk, made a cup of tea, opened a carton of milk, cooked, ate (before and after)—and always rinsed for several minutes each time. Occasionally, she would suddenly stop her work or whatever she was doing for the sole purpose of washing her hands, as though prompted by suddenly remembering some polluting occurrence or contact that necessitated washing and, inevitably, the prolonged rinsing.

The wide, shallow desk drawer was warped and had to be coaxed and jiggled open. The contents were only odds and ends—miniature ball bearing game, pennies, pencils, cracked plastic pencil sharpener, paper clips in a clump. In the closet behind the Murphy bed, a chest of drawers painted black held tangled underwear, socks, tee shirts, a pair of sweat pants, a pair of shorts. A worn pair of running shoes and a pair of black leather boots lay in the dust on the closet floor. I looked inside the medicine cabinet. As I had suspected, there were no prescription medications. The kitchen cupboards were lined with stained yellow contact paper, and their contents were few: an unscoured Revereware skillet and saucepan, unmatched dishes, a wooden salad bowl. In the drawers, a sparse and dreary litter of odd utensils.

Where were the notes? Why had she hidden them?

Outside, a door banged shut.

Lights on, water running day and night: the symptoms of personal disintegration.

I had come back, this third time, with a clear purpose. Only now, with the search frustrated, did I notice the pale object to my left, its white mass all the more conspicuous without the crouching corpse tied to it. I studied it: just an ordinary, rather old junior-size refrigerator with the freezer compartment on top.

I thought of the refrigerator at Miller Place, sleek, spotless stainless steel, two doors, a cathedral, full of food when I arrived—fresh produce, cold cuts in Nate 'n' Al's wrappers, fruit juice, milk, and in the fully stocked freezer compartment—despite the house's elaborate security system—valuable jewelry belonging to Celia's mother.

There would be no avoiding what had to come next. I would have to touch the handle of Katy's freezer compartment. I needed to steady myself because I felt nauseated again. To postpone, futilely, the moment when I would have to touch the instrument of Katy's death, I opened the refrigerator and looked inside. It was almost, but not quite empty. An apple rotted in the fruit drawer. An open package of hot-dogs on the middle shelf gave off the smell of rancid fat and garlic. A can of cherry soda, a catsup bottle, and a jar of pickle relish with a cross-threaded lid were the only other provisions on the night Katy died.

A cloud of vapor escaped when I opened the freezer compartment. The interior was coated with a thick armor of ice. When the vapor dissipated, I saw the frosted package.

It was a plastic food bag, and it tore when I pulled it away from the bottom of the compartment. In it was an insulated mailer containing a thick bunch of green 5x7 note cards covered on both sides with writing and a folder containing a photocopy of a manuscript, its pages covered with penciled notes, the title page thundering with graduate school bombast: *The Cord of Death: Fear of the Engenderer in the Films of Alfred Hitchcock.*

I went back to Katy's desk, sat down, and found the place where I'd left off reading to buy the second latté. An hour passed, then another. It was a one-sided but strangely consoling communication with my cousin who, I now felt convinced, had died hating me. I did not notice the waning of the afternoon light as the sun, obscured by clouds, dropped towards the sea. The unyielding slats of Katy's desk chair prodded my spine. It was cold, and there were rustling sounds under the floor. Katy must have heard them.

Then, I heard another sound, and it made my heart stop. From directly beneath where I sat reading, came a man's cough, rasping and wet. I held my breath and listened, but there was only the wind.

Possibly an acoustic peculiarity of the place made the cough of a passerby outside or next door sound as though it had come from under the floor. And besides, what if someone was under there? People find shelter where they can—in crawl spaces, abandoned buildings, anywhere. I shoved the papers back into the mailer, turned off the lamp, and went quickly out, stopping only to lock the door. The heavy cloud cover had brought an early dusk, and the houses and the beach glowed red in the sunset burning under the clouds.

The reconstruction of an incomplete or corrupted text calls for a special kind of imaginative effort involving empathy. It is trying to enter someone else's mind to learn that person's intention, for the fulfillment of which you become, in effect, a medium. On the surface, this may seem a selfless and even self-effacing kind of work. But it has its unwholesome side, which is like voyeurism.

I don't know for how long, unnoticed, the man followed me before the split toe of his tennis shoe appeared at my heel and discolored teeth showed in a smile of ambiguous intent. "Going my way?" he asked as he matched his pace to mine. In the last few hours, since finding the draft and notes in Katy's freezer, I had forgotten about the man in the raincoat, Stuart. Now, here he was.

I had lost myself utterly in my new project and was actually savoring the prospect of getting started. Critical bibliography may not be everyone's idea of a good time, but I had always enjoyed it: I actually felt, seeing Stuart, whom I had taken some trouble to find, a perverse if momentary disappointment at the possible opportunity of getting the lost and more complete manuscript back again, now that I'd found him, or he'd found me.

Stuart wore his raincoat over a stained UCLA hooded sweatshirt and trousers with frayed hems. He was not wearing socks.

I stopped walking. This was not the interview I had wanted, alone with him as night fell on a deserted beach.

"You wish to see me," he said quietly, raising his sun bleached eyebrows inquiringly, the eyes themselves in another mood. "A manuscript was taken." He stepped aggressively close to me. This was the impersonal aggression of the mentally ill. "*Your* manuscript?"

"No. It wasn't mine."

"But you want it," he said, not unkindly, not without irony.

"It belonged to a friend." How deftly he had put me immediately on the defensive.

He frowned and scratched inside the sweatshirt, watching me intently. The scratching seemed first to satisfy, then to irritate him. I looked away.

"You knew Kate." This was not a question, and I had to digest what it implied. He evidently had known her well enough to examine me on her behalf. Kate. I had never heard her called Kate, and his use of this name suggested a whole, vast unfamiliar dimension of her life of which my distanced neglect of her made me ignorant. Who was he?

He coughed and covered his mouth. It was a wet and sick cough.

"I'm her cousin," I said.

"She never mentioned you."

I pretended to ignore this remark, but it stung.

"Do you have her manuscript?"

He brought his face close to mine. "That's for me to know and you to find out! You are?"

I stepped back. "I would like to finish and publish her book for her."

"Did she ask you to do that?"

I did not say, No, I haven't seen her in years. I paid her no attention, even though she was having problems. I don't like a mess.

"You want to *sell* it," he persisted and watched my face. "Did *she* want to sell her work?" he quizzed, ironic on the surface, but with a disquieting undertone of suspicion. "She never mentioned you," he repeated with a subtly unpleasant emphasis as though considering the idea for the first time.

"We hadn't been in contact these last few years. But Katy was my cousin, and she was very gifted. I want to do something in her memory."

I was watching him closely, believe me. "The manuscript doesn't belong to either of us. If you don't want me to have it, there's nothing I can do. Thank you, anyway, for your time." I moved away before turning my back on him, ready to sprint if he moved suddenly.

But he wasn't listening. He was watching something on the ground.

"Who killed her, do you think?"

I stopped and turned to look at him.

Then, with a shrug and nod of resignation, he said, "It was me."

I should have gotten away then and there and called the police, but I needed to hear what he had to say. He smiled, but not at me. I could see why the counterwoman at the café hadn't wanted him around. Then, though there wasn't much light left, I saw his eyes were glistening.

"I had dinner," he said, laconically. "I was *hungry. Ich habe hunger gehabt.*"

Then he began, apparently, to re-enact something he remembered. He jabbed with his forefinger at the air. "Meatloaf. Potatoes. Peas. Bread *and* butter. A cupcake!" He smacked his lips loudly. "Yum, yum!" Then he said with un-disguised self-loathing. "I got into a van! What a time it was!"

I stood very still. I was afraid of him. I also felt the suffocating weight of my own guilt. At the troubled end of Katy's life, had this man been her only friend?

"Holy Trinity serves free meals. But it's in Santa Monica—a *long* way for me now. But yesterday, their van was in a gas station, and I got in." The lower part of his face began to twitch. "It's a long way back, but I wanted to eat. I thought I might get better if I ate." He shook his head. We both knew it would take more than a hot meal to make him better.

"But I didn't have to walk back." He opened his eyes wide, mimicking surprise. "They gave me bus fare." Again, the wracking wet cough.

"The back door was open. *She* never left it that way." His eyes filled and tears spilled onto his cheeks. "I saw her," he said, wiping his face with his sleeve. This must have been an even more horrible shock for him than it had been for me. He was so ill. But for him, there was no clean, warm bed, no one to take his temperature and make him drink his broth. "Eat, now, Stuart! Be good tonight!" No nurse, no doctor's care, no help at all.

"I was elsewhere getting my *dinner!*" he said in a voice that had dropped to a growl.

Then, something on the ground a few feet away caught his attention. With one hand holding his coat closed at his throat, he stepped away from me and bent down to pick up a chunk of doughnut.

I could have gotten away from him at that moment, the sick man, and left him far behind. But something still kept me where I stood. He straightened and brought the food to his nose. Evidently finding nothing offensive, he ate it in one bite. There were grains of sand at the corners of his mouth.

"Who are you?" His feverish eyes bored into mine.

"I'm Katy's cousin," I said again. "We were discussing her manuscript. You seem concerned about my motives."

"Ah yes. The cousin I never heard of." The corners of his mouth curved upward, but this was not a smile, and his tone was full of suspicion.

"We had been out of touch. You were a close friend of Katy's?"

"You decided to visit."

"I was invited."

"Did you phone?"

I wasn't sure what he meant. The questions and repetitions were like a maze, yet he seemed to be getting at something.

The glittering eyes that had been fixed on me looked away. Casually, he said, "I killed her." Then he leaned so close to me that I smelled fetid breath. "We all make mistakes."

He pushed his hand into a trouser pocket and pulled out a small brown leather pouch. It was an unexpectedly elegant object, glossy chestnut brown embossed with a griffin rampant. He held it up to my face and then pressed it into my hand.

"I didn't lose them *all*," he growled, spitting foam as the coughing began again, heavy, thick, and convulsive, like retching, inflaming his face and flooding his eyes with tears.

At last it subsided, but the suffering only took a different form. His chin quivered, and tears spilled from his eyes and streamed over his contorted face. He gasped for air. His nose ran freely. The coughing began yet again, this time even more punishing and violent than before. Struggling for air, he lowered himself onto the sand. When at last the fit had finished with him, he slumped forward. Now the ragged sleeve with which he wiped his face had blood on it.

"I'll get some help for you."

He waved the bloody sleeve at me. "No! I don't want them! I'll be gone when they get here. I don't need them."

I sat down beside him.

His breathing was noisy. He wiped his face with the sweatshirt hood and stared across the beach towards the ocean and the white foam of waves breaking in the dark.

I held up the pouch. "What is this?"

He was sobbing.

Inside was a yellowed newspaper clipping, a neatly cut out little rectangle. On one side was a fragment of map and on the other, what looked like part of a blotted-out advertisement. All that was legible was "ibu" on what might have been a masthead line.

I looked at Stuart, but his hands covered his face.

"What is this?" I asked him.

"Shit!" he hissed. "Everlasting shit!" Saliva collected in the corner of his mouth. He was speaking to himself, not to me, spraying drops of saliva with his words. "Fucking shit!"

Quietly, I tried again. "I don't understand. What is it?"

His tear washed face gleamed violet in the final moment of the sunset. I never saw such anguish. I put the clipping back in the pouch and stood up.

My companion stared straight ahead and did not seem to notice my going. I walked back to Washington Boulevard mulling over the possibility—reassuring, but incongruously so, under the circumstances—that after all, Katy had not written *Cantos of Malediction*.

Chapter 6

When I came in, Marlene, about to leave for the day, was massaging her hands with skin cream. The glossy, dark red enamel on her broad fingernails was undamaged after a full day's housework. She had earlier explained to me that, although she wore rubber gloves on the job for most tasks, moisture from perspiration inside the gloves caused nail polish to chip. So, to prevent this problem, she was trying something new: applying hand cream, mixed with a small amount of A & D Ointment, *before* putting on the gloves. She switched off her boom box and silenced the flood of salsa that filled the house when she worked there alone.

Marlene was not a maid. She was an independent house-cleaning contractor, as she always explained at the beginning of any business relationship. She had done so with Celia's mother, who had hired her at first sight, sensing immediately their personal compatibility and unflustered by the appearance at her door of a six-foot multi-racial transsexual in a peach colored tee shirt, ruffled at the neckline and clinging to a burly chest. Mrs. Feuerstein, had gazed in regal admiration at Marlene's well-developed leg muscles bulging in capris and recognized, with relish, that life had once again summoned her to adventure.

Now, Marlene was looking at me. "There's still some hot water here," she said with a trace of a sad smile. She poured steaming water into a large bone china cup and dropped a tea bag into it.

I felt weak and my insides hurt. I took my cup into the living room and let myself slowly down into a couch covered with rhododendrons upon which slugs and other pests did not feed. Was this real, this warm and comfortable room full of things to please the eye—the soft furniture, art, long, gray eucalyptus foliage fringing the windows, vast blanket of sparkling lights outside, fragrant tea, golden in its translucent white cup?

"I'll be back Thursday," Marlene said from the doorway as she tied the sash of her vintage 1940's jacket. "Everything OK?"

"I'm fine, thanks," I lied. "And thanks for the tea."

Marlene understood the lie. Trouble was contended with alone.

I heard her go out through the patio and pull the heavy wooden gate shut behind her.

Outside, the wind lashed the big trees against the house, and a loose pane in one of the living room windows rattled.

I wanted to talk to someone. And I wanted to be alone. The encounter with Stuart had shaken me in a way I hadn't fully grasped when I was with him and making every effort to be calm and not to agitate him. Now I was stunned at the sudden and strange intimacy I'd had with him. I had sat with him on the sand. Even now, I could almost feel and smell his breath on my face. Stuart had questioned me. "Who are you?" I was beginning to wonder about that myself.

The pouch was still in my pocket. I turned it over in my hand and looked closely at the newspaper clipping. A map and a blacked-out ad. Why had he given them to me? I went over the encounter and the uncertainties of the situation. The probable author of *Cantos of Malediction* lived beneath Katy's floor. "Who killed her, do you think?" he had asked and answered himself, "It was me." What to make of that? On the whole, I didn't believe him. The night of Katy's death the sick man had only wanted a meal, and now he seemed lacerated by guilt, as though, if only he had been with her, he might have helped her through the crisis. She might still be alive. There was no doubt in my mind that his grief and remorse were genuine. Yet, too, they could also arise from another, more sinister source.

From the table beside me came a low, purring ring.

"Bella! It's Catherine," came my old teacher's pleasant voice, an intrusion of normal life and a sudden reminder that tomorrow morning I would have to present a paper on lycanthropy and problems of judgment in Webster's plays.

"Hi," I said, and then, as though nothing out of the ordinary had happened to me, "how's the Colloquium?"

"Well as can be expected," she answered amiably. "But there's been a little hitch, you see." Silence followed. Then she said, "I'm stuck. Wonder if you could help me out a bit."

"What's wrong?"

"Well, you see...*Another* Websterian is—well, not dead—but ill. Can you believe it?"

"That's unlucky," I said.

"A back problem." She paused again. I waited for the inevitable. "So...I hate to ask, but could you possibly speak tomorrow *morning* instead of afternoon? I know how organized you are Bella, and I'm sure you could do it at this very *moment*, if need be! But tomorrow morning would be such a great help to me. The only paper that could possibly fit that slot is Angela—you know, Farrish?—and she really belongs with magic and religion on Friday."

I took a breath. "What time?"

"10:00 o'clock."

"OK."

"Knew you'd help! See you in the morning. And thanks!"

The Renaissance Colloquium! I had worked towards it and looked forward to it for months, and now it seemed a nuisance and triviality. But the truly odd thing was that I hadn't told Catherine about Katy. My cousin had committed suicide, I had found her body, and I had said nothing whatever about this personal trauma. I thought at the time that hearing Catherine's voice had made me wish that I had not gone to Venice, that I could have my normal life again as it had been before Katy's death and from which I was now barred. But there was more to it than that.

I hadn't eaten since breakfast and had no appetite. But it dawned on me at that moment that the pain in my stomach was hunger. So I thawed and heated more chicken soup in the microwave and poured a glass of milk. Then I went to the guest bathroom to wash and did not recognize the face in the malachite-framed mirror.

Chapter 7

The next morning was overcast. Another storm was coming, ushered in by high winds that lashed the trees outside against the house. The Renaissance Colloquium loomed ominously at the end of what promised to be a tense drive to San Marino in bad weather.

I washed and put on flannel trousers and a sweater. Breakfast was toast and milk. Then I put on my coat, and went out to the street through the garage, past Celia's Audi and her mother's new Jaguar.

The Feuersteins had never gotten around to selling the old Mazda bought for Marlene's predecessor. They offered me the Audi, but I decided to borrow the Mazda. I unlocked it and got in. While the engine was warming, I noticed something on the passenger seat—a manila folder, a familiar looking object.

A manila folder.

After a brief moment of staring at it I realized: the manuscript, the very thing I'd been desperate to recover, had searched for, and at last found in Ur form in Katy's freezer had spent the night in a car parked on the street! Well, high-minded plans can certainly end up being a lot of trouble, and my feelings about Katy were not uncomplicated.

After grinding the Mazda's gears, I coerced the cold and unwilling transmission into reverse and backed out of the driveway. I had to nurse the unfortunate, sputtering engine down the hill to Sunset, tailgated all the way by a black BMW with a cigar at the wheel. The houses all seemed asleep behind their tropical gardens.

By the time I arrived in San Marino, the sky had darkened, and big raindrops began to fall just as I reached the Library entrance, overwhelmed by the sense that leaving the manuscript in the car overnight expressed me to perfection: I had been lying to myself again.

I joined the Jacobean section of the Colloquium in a handsome old room paneled in dark oak with an aged but well-preserved green carpet and graceful Edwardian furnishings. As I stood in the doorway, a corpulent figure separated itself from a group of scholars waiting for the call to be seated. Joseph Hruska had been in graduate school with me. He came towards me, arms outstretched and wearing a broad smile of welcome. "Well!" he said taking my hands and looking me over. He was appraising my expensive clothes.

"Still gorgeous!"

I am not gorgeous. He meant the Armani pants and sweater and whatever ungorgeous things I'd done to pay for them.

I smiled back. "You're looking good yourself, Joe."

It was true. He was large and fat, but also robust. Despite his weight, he was an agile and energetic squash player, an experienced outdoorsman, and a certified whitewater guide. He was legendary for having walked from Berkeley to Ashland for the Shakespeare Festival. He read well in five languages—two ancient and three modern—and, in fact, never stopped reading. He also had an unequaled and well-earned reputation for backbiting.

"I heard about your book," I said, "congratulations! But where are you now?"

"Rutgers."

"Aha."

There was silence. Then, he said, "Speaking today, I see. Thought you'd gone on to—uh—onwards and upwards."

"I'm not teaching now, so in a way, you're right. Catherine needed some Webster for this morning. Someone couldn't make it."

"Graeme. He's getting too old for B and D in the Low Countries." He glanced resentfully at Professor Frankenstaad, who stood across the room chatting animatedly with another woman. Surely there were other Websterians who could have taken Graeme's place, Websterians who had kept themselves current!

"I liked your Kyd book," I said, calling him back. "Read it last year."

He smiled gratefully, and I remembered what had been so difficult about him. He was the most striking mixture of genuine good will and sheer nastiness I'd ever met. I had never been ready for either aspect of his nature.

Catherine crossed the room. Her face was fantastically like a frog's, and she had a thin-limbed, plump-torsoed body to match. She kissed my cheek with a loud smack.

"Oh, boy, am I glad to see you!" Her face was flushed. As usual, she looked as though she thought everything, even her own difficulties, rather funny. "This has been a nightmare, of course," she said with evident enjoyment. "Everything has gone wrong, as I expected. How I got into this I don't know!" She glanced at Joseph without acknowledging his presence. "You won't believe the refreshments. At least I didn't order them for outside! But I never saw a more depressing selection of canapés! Ugh!"

The famous scholar's frizzy black hair was drawn back into a small bun out of which stuck, as always, unruly hairs like wires. With the usual lack of success, she tried to smooth them as she walked to the front of the room where two long walnut tables had been arranged end to end with water pitchers and glasses on them.

As the forty or so men and women found their seats, I and the other speakers took our places at the tables facing the group. Catherine introduced us. She was completely at ease and spoke as though introducing old friends over lunch.

Immediately, as boded ill for my presentation, my thoughts began to wander. I found myself thinking about Stuart and his life before illness and the streets had claimed him. There must have been a time when he had lived and worked like other people, had dinner with friends, driven a car, gone to the movies...

"...the King James Bible in relation to Jacobean tragic drama. Then, on escapism in Stuart historical drama, Wayne Baumgartner of the University of Virginia," she smiled with a trace of affection at a gaunt gray haired man who returned the smile. "And, Joanna Bowers..."

Could I find Stuart again? How much time did he have left?

The listeners shifted in their leather armchairs, preparing for the approaching test of their collective stamina.

"I'm sorry to tell you that Al Graeme has been under the weather in Amsterdam and won't arrive until tomorrow. In his place this morning is Bella Marx, formerly of the University of California, Berkeley, with a new look at Webster's non-dramatic models."

It was a great relief to see that several members of this rather distinguished audience actually appeared interested in my topic. Catherine had stopped talking and was looking at me. She had not told me that I would be speaking first.

Reasonably good delivery got me through. I remembered how to do this, not rushing, attending to my own words, from time to time looking up. Afterwards, there were questions, including a strident attempt at a deconstructionist interpretation, which surprised me, because I would have thought that by now, deconstructionism had gone the way of other fads of literary criticism. An elderly woman brought in Italian comedy and spoke at length, making some of the listeners grimace and squirm.

Professor Morgan, a Tourneur specialist, spoke next. From the estate of a Dorsetshire nobleman, he had acquired the diary of a contemporary of Tourneur, which, he explained for about three quarters of an hour, had conclusively established that Tourneur had written *The Revenger's Tragedy*: "only a complete and damned degenerate rogue [like Tourneur] could have written the filthy graveyard scene." This was the evidence. As an endnote, Professor Morgan related in detail the history of his acquisition of the diary, discovered in a children's nursery chest stuffed with sheets of music, toys, and other odds and ends. He read without once looking up from his papers. The men and women in the audience listened intently. (Professor Morgan was Editor-in-Chief of *Studies in Renaissance Literature.*)

The other panelists read their work. The last question was asked and responded to. There was applause, and Catherine hurried out to check on the refreshments. However unappealing, they would be devoured and disparaged.

I collected my papers and opened my folder to put them inside with Katy's manuscript, which I had brought into the Library with me. This time I had not been careless.

Alfred Hitchcock, Artist of the Unconscious stood out on the title page. I read it a second time, after which I had an absolutely clear and perfect recollection of arriving back at Miller Place the previous night, carefully locking both doors of the Mazda, and carrying everything I had brought from Katy's into the house with me.

On the polished walnut table was the manuscript that had disappeared from my table at the Café Bougainville in Venice.

Chapter 8

The streets back to the Harbor Freeway were lined with old liquidambars. I kept my eye on the road and avoided the distraction of the dazzlingly colored trees with their masses of red and orange foliage against the slate-dark sky. To me they suggested the wonderful contrasts of autumn—outdoors, impending cold, shortening days, leaves in the air and under foot; indoors, a world of comfortable snugness, glowing fireplaces, fruit pies laced with cinnamon and other spices, provisions against the dead time of year—the autumn that I had never experienced growing up.

Traffic on the freeway was heavy and racing through torrential rain that began as soon as I cleared the on-ramp. The Mazda's windshield wipers wagged frantically back and forth, and Alfred Hitchcock, Artist of the Unconscious rode in the passenger seat. Tucked in its pages was the postcard I'd sent earlier that year to Celia from France and which I had used at the café to mark my place in the manuscript. Stuart must have used it to find me. The trip by bus from Venice to West

Hollywood must have been a harsh ordeal for the sick man, or had someone else made the delivery?

"I don't talk to him," the counter woman had said. "And you don't want to find him."

Now he had found me for the second time. And why? He mistrusted me and found my motives suspect. Why, then, return the manuscript to which he had seemed to think I had no right. Had he belatedly realized my sincerity? Or was it, rather, that he wanted me to know that he could find me—he or a friend of his?

I reached the Laurel Canyon exit at about 2:30. The Mazda made the climb to Mulholland Drive, but, to judge from the temperature gage, under protest. On the downhill heading into West Hollywood, the generator light went on and stayed on, glowing ominously on the dashboard like a bloodstain. Turning onto Sunset Boulevard, I saw a gas station and pulled up to the repair bay.

A short, dark, Middle Eastern-looking man in a yellow slicker came towards the car, and I rolled down the window.

"My generator light is on," I said without other greeting. "It's been on since Mulholland."

The man shook his head. "Pop the hood."

He looked at the steaming engine. "Miss," he admonished, "you almost got no fan belt."

"How much to replace it?"

"$12.50 for the belt. Plus labor."

"How much is that?"

"$169.70 per hour."

This was LA. I could call Triple A for a tow, but I'd still have to find a shop to replace the belt.

"You drive like this all the way from Mulholland?"

"Yes."

"You overheat."

"The engine *was* hot."

He sighed. "Maybe your block cracked."

Even I knew this was a serious problem.

"How long will it take to find out?"

"Don't worry. Maybe not so bad. I see."

$169.70 per hour. "How long will it take to find out?" I asked again.

"Well," he gestured towards the service bay, "I got some cars aheada you already."

The bay was indeed full.

"Tomorrow, 4:00, maybe."

"Could you possibly make it sooner—tonight or in the morning?"

"I don't work nights," he replied with dignity.

"No. I see." Could the insult be forgiven? I found a twenty dollar bill in my purse, and he took it with a deft, almost imperceptible gesture.

"You call later—5:00. Ask for Bob."

I left the key in the ignition, wrapped my work and Katy's papers in a plastic bag that I found in the trunk, and started west on Sunset Boulevard in a downpour that veiled the boutiques, record stores, clubs, and cafés along the curving street. A bus pulled away from its stop just as I got there. Cars rushed by, but there were no cabs and, this being LA, probably no more buses for a long time.

I stepped into the shelter. My pale gray Italian loafers—stupidly chosen given the weather outlook that morning—were now black. The Armani pants were saturated.

I pushed my soaked hair back from my face and started out again. Miller Drive, which led uphill to Miller Place, was only about a half a mile away, but the distance seemed a lot longer than it had that morning going in the opposite direction by car. There were puddles everywhere. Crossing the street was downright frightening, and it was impossible not to be splashed by cars tearing by. I looked—and was—pathetic.

I reached Miller Drive in about a quarter of an hour and started up the hill, slogging past the Mediterranean style houses and their big-leafed, flowering plants and heavily foliaged trees swaying and shaking in the wind. Occasionally, a passing car lost traction on the steep, wet street.

Sweating and drenched, I reached Celia's house and used my key to open the heavy wooden gate set into the high stucco wall that enclosed a flagstone patio in a small jungle of bougainvilleas, oleanders, and tree ferns. I let myself into the house and dripped water on the floor. It was quiet. I could hear the soft click of the kitchen wall clock as the hands advanced. I thought of Stuart in the crawlspace under Katy's apartment, finding me at the beach and at Miller Place, and unlocking the Mazda. Still in my wet clothes, I went to check the doors.

I had locked the front door behind me when I came inside. Now I dropped the brass floor bolt in place. The garage door was locked, and so was the kitchen door leading to the garage. I checked the doors leading out onto the deck and those downstairs leading to the garden. All the windows were locked. I armed the alarm system. Then, I pulled off my wet clothes, put them in the laundry room, and went back downstairs for a shower. After that I called Bob. He reported gloomily that the only problem was the fan belt, and that would be fixed by 10:00 AM.

Again, chicken soup and milk, but this time, I barely got them down.

The Colloquium was finished, but there were other things to do. In addition to the burial arrangements, I'd also have to notify Katy's employer and return the submissions. There were two FedEx mailers. In one were two outlines, two screenplays, a treatment, a typed memo to Katy, and an airbill pre-addressed to the Bass Joseph Agency. In the other mailer were a single treatment and a note from Katy: "Zoe—who is G.M. Knapp? K."

Once during her time as a film editor, Katy told me a story about a young man who accosted a famous director at an airport and shoved a screenplay into his hand. The director had, it turned out, liked the story, but couldn't find the young man because he hadn't included his contact information in the manuscript. Intrigued, I picked up the treatment which, like the one in Katy's story, had no return address. But this was not a story treatment.

Chapter 9

The Hatchet Man by G.N.Knapp
San Francisco, 1873

The night is clear, and the cold is sharpened by wind blowing from the northwest. Streets and shop windows are decorated with winter greenery. Some of the horses wear decorated harnesses.

But Chinatown is not part of San Francisco New Year's Eve. The room in which the young man stands is its own world. Wo Han is sixteen years old. His thin, oval face is expressionless and his physique slender. He is unnoticed standing in the near darkness, breathing in smoke and the odors of stale clothing and unwashed bodies. In the bunk beds are both men and women.

"Wo Mai." He speaks the name softly, yet loudly enough to be heard over the murmuring in the room. The searching seems futile, and if she were here among these bodies, would she answer him? Would she recognize her own name? He walks along the rows of bunks and examines the faces.

There is a sailor with a badly bruised face; a middle aged blonde woman in green velvet; a dark-skinned Malay, shirtless and barefoot in trousers too short for his long legs, scars on his ankles and wrists; a small, frail looking albino gazing at Wo Han with unfocused eyes. Wo Han studies every face and recognizes none.

One smoker is a richly dressed Mandarin. Wo Han notices a sash of black silk lying on the rough wood floor beside his bunk. It is somehow familiar. In his mind there is an image of such a serpent-like and hated thing. Now comes the pain in his head for which there is no remedy.

A hand lightly touches his arm. The old woman who dispenses the drug from her place at a small table at one end of the room has approached him and looks inquiringly into his face.

"Do you know Wo Mai?" he asks her.

The old woman smiles showing brown teeth and shrugs.

Wo Han walks from the room. The door is closed behind him. The passageway in which he stands is in total darkness. He must feel his way as he goes. He gropes at the wall and eases his way around a corner. He stumbles over something soft and unseen. He hears the steps of someone running, but he meets no one.

At last, a faint light appears ahead. He walks faster now. The darkness is no longer absolute, and the damp, stale, bad-smelling air unnerves and sickens him. There are two steps up to a door at whose edges he can see light from outside. He pulls open the door and steps out of the labyrinth into narrow, gas-lit Commercial Street.

Wo Han shivers in his cotton clothing. His body aches with fatigue.

The work in the laundry begins every day before dawn and lasts into evening. He has little time to search for his mother, from whom he was separated months ago at Angel Island. Since arriving in San Francisco, the young man has searched Chinatown restaurants and other business establishments of every kind. He has questioned relentlessly, but no one knows or has seen the woman with the scar over her left eye.

The night after his visit to the opium room, his long day at the laundry at an end, Wo Han plods through the mud of Pacific Avenue. Tonight, feeling unwell and exhausted, he thinks only of rest. Suddenly, there is commotion. A dry goods store on DuPont Street is on fire. People with pails of water try to douse the flames; others try to save what they can from the burning building. The smoke filled street is crowded with onlookers.

To avoid the crowds and the dense smoke, Wo Han turns from his usual route home onto Washington Street and walks north on Montgomery, where three American sailors have appeared suddenly on the street as if by magic. They are laughing. Wo Han watches them as they walk away together towards Market Street.

The door through which they came is a few steps below the level of the street. It is unlit. To find his mother, he must look everywhere, no matter how bad the place. So he goes in.

The candlelit room smells of wood smoke from a stove in one corner. The floor is bare. Heavy footsteps echo behind the curtain veiling a doorway that leads to a corridor.

The room is furnished with a bench, a table with candles flickering on it, and a chair in which sits a woman of indeterminate age. Her emaciated body and damp-looking hair are at odds with her traditional Chinese gown of gold brocade. She sips tea and welcomes the young man with a wan and knowing smile.

He hands her what money he has—just a few coins—and asks about his mother, mentioning the scar.

"Ah, yes," says the woman. "Such a person was here. But her name was Jew Mai. She did not stay long," the woman added with a ghastly toothless smile.

"*Jew* Mai?" Wo Han is puzzled. The name is wrong. "Jew Mai? You are certain?"

The woman nods.

"She went to the Asylum."

Wo Han does not understand.

"A place for insane. Past the dunes. There are wolves."

She drinks tea. "A name is of no importance."

Her fleshless hand pours out more of the steaming brew. Without looking up, she says, "Insane inside prisons" and shakes her head slowly.

Wo Han feels fear creeping over him. Yet, he will continue to search.

"What if you found her *here*?" the woman asks, leering. "Would she be happy to see you?"

Wo Han turns to leave as a gigantic sailor comes in. Wo Han hears the sound of coins falling onto the table.

The next night, he begins the long walk westward on California Street, past large houses with golden light shining from their windows, past the western edge of San Francisco, into the dark. Again, it is necessary to climb. If good luck continues, he will meet no unruly white men.

He is not strong, and the long, hard walk makes breathing difficult. It is cold, but he perspires heavily.

Into his mind comes the noise of the crowd and the odors of fish, roasting meat, and cow dung. All of a sudden, people are pushed forcibly back, jostling and treading on each other. Wo Han, a child, is pulled back into the throng.

The Mandarin's men are clearing a path through the market: their master wishes to pass. The people move submissively back to make way. A hush falls, for no one wants to attract the attention of the Mandarin's men. A riding crop is raised aloft and snaps downward. The midday summer sun is scorching hot.

The fish seller does not for a moment relax his grip on the little boy's small arm. When the procession has passed, he drags Wo Han to his stall. Wo Han's mother is there. A few minutes earlier, she had stood laughing with the fish seller. Now her face is diagonally bisected by a gleaming red slash. Time has brought Wo Han no relief from the pain of this memory.

At the crest of the hill, he meets an even sharper, colder wind. He passes the graveyards. The dead will not harm him.

Now there are dunes. The terrain is unfamiliar. He has never before traveled so far to the west. Occasionally, a light glimmers in the darkness. Shacks are scattered about in the dunes. A co-worker has told him that California Street leads to the sea, but none of those whom he asked knew the location of the Asylum; few even knew of its existence.

Wo Han stops and peers into the black distance at what seem to be tiny and faint pinpoints of light. He starts towards them and eventually arrives at a large brick structure on a high bluff overlooking the sea. Its small windows are barred and its double doors

K. M. WOOD

are made of heavy metal. An iron bell hangs
beside them. Wo Han pulls its cord and asks
the nun who appears for Wo Mai.

She looks Wo Han over, but does not answer.
Wo Han then asks for Jew Mai. He repeats both
names several times and explains the purpose
of his visit, but in Chinese. The nun leads
him to a guarded anteroom. Jew Mai is brought
in. She has a long scar on her face, but it is
on her cheek, not across her eye. She bears no
resemblance to Wo Han's mother, although the
young man feels that he has seen her before.

At the sight of Wo Han, Jew Mai stands perfectly still, her head tilted to one side, her
eyes staring fixedly at the floor. Then, she
kneels on all fours and, crawling backwards,
moves to the door through which she has just
been led and begins a clumsy series of back-
ward kicks on it.

Wo Han is soaked with perspiration.

"Ramon!" the nun calls out.

A gangling Mexican boy comes in, lifts Jew
Mai to her feet and leads her, still staring
at the floor, back into the inner recesses of
the Asylum.

"Punished for wickedness," the nun murmurs.

Now, the darkness outside is comforting,
and Wo Han is glad to leave this frightful

place, glad that he did not find his mother inside. Shaken, he walks to the edge of the bluff inhaling the fresh night air from the sea. He sits listening to the moaning of the wind in the cypress trees and the low roar of the waves below. Far away to the west is his homeland.

He remembers the brothel keeper's face as she told him that this was the right place for the Asylum. She had smiled at him as though he should understand some veiled meaning in her words.

Why, he wonders, do white men punish mad people? Madness is itself a punishment for offending ancestors, and ancestors punish without pity. Why, in this strange place, do the living add their cruelty to the vengeance of ancestors?

Dense fog shrouds land and water. Wo Han is deeply chilled. But from sheer exhaustion caused by the long trek from Chinatown and the disturbing experience with the madwoman, he falls asleep in the shelter of thick cypress branches. Waking some hours later, he can see shapes moving about on the beach below where he sits. The dead, demons, spirits, Asylum inmates escaped from confinement: what they are, he cannot tell. They prowl the beach from water to land and then seem to disappear into the bluff.

He is afraid. Rising to his feet, he rushes back across the dunes in stumbling flight, laboring forward, gasping and out of breath, his progress constrained by the sand. At long last, he gains the road and is relieved to feel its hard surface beneath his weakened legs. His feet pound against it in soft-soled slippers filled with sand.

Again he passes the cemeteries, and this time he hears revelers. They are invisible in the fog. These are white men's voices, but now, Wo Han is reassured by the nearness of other people and by the glow of light from the city that grows nearer.

He arrives home shivering and stiff from cold. The soles of his feet are sore and burning. In the dark, he spreads his bed mat on the floor and covers himself with his blanket. His sleep is sound until he is visited by someone neither man nor woman. Faded yellow garments drape the skeletal body. The eyes are clouded. Across one eye is a long scar. The figure beckons to Wo Han as he walks on a beach. The sun is at its zenith, but its light is dim, as during an eclipse. Wo Han wants to escape, but he is drawn forward towards the figure and towards the water and mountainous surf.

He has had this dream before. Always at the water's edge, he wakes, breathing hard, relieved to find that that he has been dreaming. Again, he sleeps, undisturbed by the door that rattles, even though the wind has died.

The following evening, arriving home, Wo Han sees a thin vertical beam of dim lamplight: the door of the shack is slightly ajar. On the single chair sits a man whom Wo Han has never before seen.

"Wo Han," the man says, his clean-shaven face smiling genially. He does not rise.

Wo Han bows, sensing too late that it is a mistake to enter his home with the stranger there.

The man then stands and offers the chair to his host, who declines. A courteous altercation ensues, and Wo Han at last is seated. The stranger then walks to the door and bolts it. Unfastening his jacket, he reveals a small hatchet at his waist.

The young man is too frightened to speak. To whom has he given offense?

The stranger explains that he dislikes being the cause of suffering. In fact, his diet consists only of vegetables and grains. Even to the detriment of his professional reputation, he will consider allowing Wo Han to live in exchange for information.

Wo Han is so frightened that he is barely able to nod his assent.

"Last night, you were at the sea."

Wo Han again nods. His mind is in turmoil. What does the stranger want of him?

"Why did you go to that place?"

Wo Han is shivering now from fear. "I am searching for my mother," is his barely audible reply.

Suddenly he understands. The shapes on the beach—they were real people! Perhaps they were being put ashore without the blessing of the law. Slaves!

"Was anyone with you?"

Wo Han shakes his head. He must save himself. If the man knows that Wo Han was on the bluff, he must have been there, as well. He must know that the shapes on the beach were visible from above.

"There were spirits. That is a terrible place."

The stranger closes his eyes in sympathy. "Only spirits."

Wo Han has correctly discerned the man's intention: to learn whether there were other witnesses to the slave smuggling.

"I saw no *living* person. I am certain."

"Thank you for assisting me," the man says. "Naturally, when questioning the nun at the Asylum, it was necessary for me to explain that you are my deranged nephew suffering from delusions about his deceased mother."

Wo Han stares at the man who has bound him in a fiction.

Wo Han's hand moves to his head. The pain is returning, and this in itself is a cause for fear.

The man draws a black length of silk cord from his blouse. "This kind of cord was used to murder Wo Mai."

Wo Han's mind reels. The pain in his head is blinding.

The man smiles in a knowing and admonitory way. "You have no memory of Jew Mai?"

Had he seen the woman before his visit to the Asylum? He has no memory of his last days in Shanghai.

"That is curious. She has not forgotten you, from Shanghai. You did not see her watching as you strangled Wo Mai."

Now the small hatchet is in the man's hand. Wo Han knows that an assassin's weapon, once drawn, means death.

Although knowing himself condemned, and despite the pain in his head, he asks, "Will you not, then, allow me to live?" He is careful not to imply that the man is about to break his word.

"Nephew," the man replies softly, "my words were that I would *consider* allowing you to live." After a silence, he concludes, "This I have done."

From Shantung, there came a young couple. They lived in the shack after Wo Han's death. The wife scrubbed for many hours using precious hot water, but she could not remove the ugly stain from the floorboards. She placed a table over it. Now the shack contained two chairs. She and her husband forgot about the stain. The shack had a good roof, and the walls were without holes.

1615

And the walls were without holes. And there were no holes in the walls.

Katy and I had debated which of these two would work best. I don't remember which one we had finally chosen.

For a prize of fifty dollars and honor, in one night in Stern Hall, we two freshmen created our entry for the *Daily Cal* Annual Short Story Contest. Our entry did not win, but we weren't especially disappointed. We had fun writing it, eating Mallomars and drinking illegally gotten beer, with the cold, clear, black night outside and the lights of San Francisco in the distance until the sun came up. I still am not sure at what point I recognized that what I was reading in Mrs. Feuerstein's kitchen was the story that Katy and I wrote that night.

PART 2

At Home

Chapter 10

"The Hatchet Man" had begun to haunt me. Whoever had reworked the story must have had fun, rendering the action in the present tense to make it look like an actual story treatment, roping the reader in. This was a feline sort of fun—the play with quarry that preceded the kill, the misleading and bizarre semblance of camaraderie with the predator. In "The Hatchet Man" I saw a jeering exhibitionism and the hand of a trickster. Even I, as I read, had been drawn into the narrowing passageway of the story which, the more I recognized its lineaments, the more clearly I recalled that retributive justice and personal moral responsibility were not part of the story my cousin and I had written.

I began to understand the revisions made by G.N. Knapp to our narrative. Their purpose, clearly, was to allow the writer to define a role for himself with respect to the reader. I am someone you wouldn't suspect—a would-be screenwriter with an interest in San Francisco history and preparing a story treatment in the usual way. But you are to understand, my story has a special significance for one reader in particular. I am closer than you think.

There was even menace in the present tense verbs, used in the usual manner of story treatments, but here asserting that the events of the narrative exist in the real and extra-literary present. We had called our story "The Dead Do No Harm." The game designed by G.N. Knapp for Katy—in which I, too, now was involved—invited discernment of some latent fact or detail, like a composition of hidden pictures. It was clear to me that I was missing something.

At the westernmost end of the black mass presented in the dark by the Marin Headlands, the Point Bonita light-house flashed its beacon like a diamond. To the east, the Bridge was outlined in festive orange lights. My back yard, like those of the other houses along that stretch of Seacliff Avenue, ended at the edge of the cliff that drops down to Baker Beach. My husband had grown up in that house, and his family had liked to swim in the frigid water there, outside the Golden Gate. A narrow, steep flight of wood stairs gave access to the beach. But time and weather had brought them decay, and I had not made repairs. Though I liked the easy access down, it no longer seemed a good idea to provide it going up.

The house has three stories, the uppermost of which, af-ter Alan died, I converted to an apartment for myself. The lower floors I rented to a Japanese investment banker and his family and by this arrangement reconciled two powerful and opposing needs: to leave behind the house that I loved and its ghosts, on the one hand, and on the other, to stay. Each choice was as painful as not deciding between them.

On the water below, the lights of a departing ship glimmered in the darkness. The last time I stood here looking down, Katy was alive.

Three gleaming, brown drops of Mongolian Beef sauce had spattered onto the glass coffee table across which my sister-in-law, wearing an indigo Chanel suit, watched me eat. Aliza had been sitting in the beautiful suit on my doorstep when I arrived home late that afternoon, beside her a container of Mongolian Beef just showing at the top of a large bag of groceries.

"Uh oh," was all she said when she saw me.

She turned on the heat and some lights, called home to tell her son to walk the dog, and waited while I showered.

"Has it been raining much?"

"Yes. How about a walk tomorrow? I could make time."

"Like to, but I have to take care of something."

"The funeral arrangements?"

"That, too. But I have to go to Berkeley."

Aliza nodded. That meant a visit to my father's house.

"What's up?"

"I want to go through some papers."

She watched me. "How're you feeling?"

"Well enough, I guess. I thought I was getting a cold, but didn't. I'm tired, though."

I knew what she was thinking. Tired and run down—natural enough— found a dead cousin, how was the weather, business as usual tomorrow.

Here was the cardinal sin of emotional denial. Where was the response to the trauma? To the awful job of mopping up, arranging for the shipment of the body and for the funeral, dealing with loss? Aliza, who never undervalued her own judgment, was the best of friends. But the difficulty one faced with her was her insistence that catharsis occur in the approved form—that of the open, not necessarily pleasant, discussion of feelings.

"I'm so sorry, Bel," she said.

I looked across the Mongolian Beef at my husband's sister and my close friend.

"Did you tell Roger?"

I nodded.

"You know, I could stay over tonight. Always did like this couch."

"I'm OK."

"Scary thing, finding a dead person."

"That wasn't the scariest part. I didn't tell you everything over the phone. I found out some disturbing things."

"Like what?"

"She wasn't taking medication."

"Oh my. Well, that would explain a lot. In that kind of situation, causes and effects can be rather mixed up with each other."

"I think she wanted me to be the one to find her."

"What do you mean?"

"Everything seemed arranged. I mean, she invited me over, and we agreed, as I told you, on a time, but when I arrived, no one was there—or so I thought—but the door was open, and the light was on—the one light—and even though the place was a mess, which I expected, because Katy always was rather a slob, the desk was perfectly neat—that also was not unexpected—but a book that I had given her was placed prominently in the middle, and work that she had finished was ready to be sent out."

If I wanted credibility, and I did, this blurting style of delivery was not the best way to achieve it. Aliza looked as though someone had told her a joke and left out the punch line. She neither challenged nor wanted explanation. What would be the point? She saw wear and tear for which a good dinner, sleep, and distance from traumatic events were indicated therapies.

"Well, OK, but if she had arranged things, as you say, would it be surprising? People who kill themselves are angry and, you know, unbalanced. They are not the people whose judgments we rely on. And if I remember correctly, the rejection was mutual."

This was true, but it made me feel worse. I was telling her too much. Should I have told her about Stuart and his confession of guilt which I, too, could have made? About Stuart living under Katy's apartment, or paying a visit in the night—himself or through another—to Miller Place with Katy's manuscript?

I could imagine Aliza's reaction, quiet and on full alert. What did the police think about that? Let me guess: you didn't tell them about the deranged street person who said he killed your cousin.

I didn't seriously suspect that events had been other than they seemed. Katy had committed suicide. I would know by now if she had not, if someone had murdered her. The police would know by now. What I wanted to find out was what had led to the decision to die, and this was not a police matter.

Stuart had delivered Katy's manuscript to Miller Place, or someone had delivered it for him. Someone had picked the lock of the Mazda as it sat in the driveway and had done the job skillfully and left no noticeable sign of forced entry. Stuart was more than he seemed—a pathetic man ravaged by illness and probably drugs—but illness could mask capabilities better for his purpose not generally known. On my way to the airport, I had gone again to Venice.

I went to the Café, looked for him on the beach, and went back to Katy's apartment building. I looked in the crawlspace where someone lay covered by newspapers. A foul odor permeated the close atmosphere of the place.

"Stuart," I said, but only once. Whoever it was did not respond. The smell was intolerable.

"I went through Katy's papers, and I found a manuscript," I said. "I realized that she must have been writing a book, and then it dawned on me that I might be able to finish it for her, you see, and have it published. Then maybe I'd feel better about what a rotten friend I had been."

"I don't think you were a rotten friend."

I smiled at the kindness and wondered if the gap that was opening between us was to be permanent.

"Katy had finished some story evaluations and I thought I should return her work to the agent, her employer. It was all packaged and ready to go, as though she had left them for me. But there was one with no address. I read that one."

"What did you do with it?"

"I brought it back with me."

"It's their problem, isn't it—the agent's, I mean. Why didn't you just send it back with the others?"

"Because I wrote it."

She looked blank.

"I mean, Katy and I wrote it together in college. We entered it in a short story contest. I don't know how it arrived on Katy's desk, but what I read was our story, with some changes. Someone must have sent it to her."

"That's interesting. Not necessarily. But why couldn't she have had it all along. Maybe she was rewriting it…thought she could sell it, or something."

"We wrote it such a long time ago. We were just fooling around. It wasn't published. The originals weren't returned to people, you know. We had a copy, but I'm almost positive that I kept it."

"But you don't remember for sure. And anyway, when you think about it, she could have known lots of people and exchanged projects with folks, and so on."

"It was such a peculiar, oddball little story, and I can't imagine someone else—just coincidentally—writing the same one."

"This was exactly the same story?"

"No, not exactly. There were some changes in the language—everything changed to the present tense, for instance—and a new theme."

"So, it wasn't the same."

"It was about a young Chinese immigrant laundry worker in early San Francisco who was searching for his mother."

"So what are you suggesting?"

"I don't know. Was someone helping her to disintegrate?"

"Bella, mentally ill people kill themselves sometimes. You know this. The police can tell the difference between suicide and other kinds of death. They would have told you if it was, well, not suicide. And you know what? If you could remember the story, so could Katy. She could have rewritten it from memory."

"It was in a FedEx mailer from an agency," I said.

"For heaven's sake. Maybe she reused mailers. I do that. Do we even know that this story actually *arrived* in the mailer?"

Good point. I hadn't checked. "Not for sure, but there was a note from Katy inside asking about the author, who, incidentally, didn't provide a return address."

Aliza said nothing.

"Another thing, Aliza. That story had strange footers."

She looked perfectly calm, even relaxed, drinking tea. I wasn't fooled. She was worried about me and upset. I should never have tried to explain.

"And?"

"There were two of them, one on the odd numbered pages, the other on the even numbered ones. *Rev* on the odd-numbered pages, and *1615* on the even. I use footers in my own work, you know, for identifying manuscripts, and numbering pages, indicating drafts, and so on. At first I thought Rev could mean revision. But why alternate? And what about *1615*? As a date, it had no relevance that I could recognize to the story. I had never used alternating footers and don't even know what they're for."

"I don't either," Aliza said quietly.

"Then I put them together."

Aliza leaned forward and poured us both more tea.

I didn't continue immediately. For some reason, predominant at that moment, among all the disparate and painful reactions to those last few days, was the thought of the long distance conversation with my father, during which, not to my surprise, he avoided helping with the funeral and shipping arrangements by using the familiar excuse which no one believed, but neither was it ever questioned, of ill health.

"'Behold, I come as a thief.'"

"What's that?"

"That's what I found when I put the footers together. It's from the Bible. It's Revelation, chapter 16, verse 15. Revelation is the last book of the New Testament."

"Ah. Behold, what?"

"Behold, I come as a thief."

"And what does that mean, actually?"

"Well, Revelation is difficult and obscure, even for a Scriptural book. For one thing, although the translators produced great English prose, their Greek may not have been sound. But, at any rate, the passage in question doesn't make clear who the speaker is, and the ambiguity has to be intentional, although a strong candidate is one of seven angels who are agents of God. The book is apocalyptic, and the statement—Behold, I come as a thief—in or out of context, is unmistakably sinister."

"That's a different angle," Aliza remarked with a smile. "Isn't that on the blasphemous side? Not that I mean to disagree, but it's not a widely held view—is it?—that God is sinister."

"I was thinking that it had to do with reversals—the overturning of moral values in the errant or corrupt soul, with Divine Agency seen as a kind of menace."

She grimaced. "Bella, have you taught this book?"

"As a matter of fact, yes. But that doesn't make me wrong. Anyway, I'm driving over to Roger's tomorrow. I'll see if any of my things from college are still there, in the garage, maybe. I had some boxes of old papers. Maybe the story is in one of them."

"Look, Bel," Aliza began in a gentler tone than usual, "I think there's more than one thing going on here. What, really, do you expect to find out tomorrow at Roger's? If the story's there, if it's not there—so what? You don't really know what it was that you read. Maybe Katy rewrote from memory the story you wrote together. Maybe—who knows—she shared it with the wrong person, and that person stole her idea and, by sheer coincidence, sent it to the agent that Katy worked for. That could be the reason for the note and, by the way, seems much more likely than that someone—whoever— was using it to do mischief.

"You know," she went on, "when people die, we can't bring them back. We also can't make amends for some things. We're just limited that way. Maybe for you—and for me— this compulsive searching for causes and explanations is a way of trying to have some measure of control when, in fact, we have very little. It's no use trying, and I think it's harmful.

"Katy fought depression for years. From what you told me, she had other problems, too. She finally simply wasn't able to cope any more. This is a terrible thing, but it was not your fault."

She paused and looked down at her hands, turning the narrow, gold wedding band with pavé diamonds in it. "I always feel apologetic when I talk to you about yourself. It seems like presuming. I'm sorry. But you need to get back to work and live your life. In the process of knocking yourself out to undo what has been done and sealed and chasing after what you can't possibly have, you'll miss the chance to get back some of what you lost when Alan died. You have writing. You have friends who love you. You even have a chance to get back into teaching—you told me, remember?"

She was right.

Aliza and I knew each other well, and I was not surprised when she brought up Syd, my psychiatrist, and asked if I'd be seeing him any time soon. I answered, yes, that was a good idea.

Chapter 11

When she had gone, I did the dishes.

As undergraduates, Katy and I were zealous political moralists. Our story, if it had any purpose at all, was intended to illuminate social evils. Our Wo Han never found his mother and never learned her fate. He was merely a victim of greed, and his death was a mere business necessity brought about to protect the slaving operation onto which he had accidentally stumbled. In G.N. Knapp's version, he was a deranged matricide whose death had about it overtones of retributive justice.

I found my King James Bible in the hallway bookcase and took it to bed with me.

And I heard a great voice out of the temple saying to the seven angels, Go your ways, and pour out the vials of the wrath of God upon the earth./And the first went, and, so did they all, until the sixth poured out his vial upon the great river Euphrates; and the water thereof was dried up, that the way of the kings of the east might be prepared./ And I saw three unclean beasts like frogs come out of the mouth of the dragon, and out of the mouth of the beast, and out of the mouth of the false prophet./For they are the spirits of devils, working miracles, which go forth unto the kings of the earth and of the whole world, to gather them to the battle of that great day of God Almighty./ Behold, I come as a thief. Blessed is he that watcheth, and keepeth his garments, lest he walk naked, and they see his shame./And he gathered them together into a place called in the Hebrew tongue Armageddon...

Here was the hallucinatory, mind-exploding vision of St. John the Divine with its intricate fabric of peripeteia and transformations. Only the most searching view of life produced moral valuation like this one. At first sight, "Behold, I come as a thief" had seemed menacing enough. In its context, with the culminating invocation of Armageddon, it reverberated with the terrible authority of divine wrath. It wasn't until I read this passage that I recognized this same intention, though crudely and ludicrously realized, in *Cantos of Malediction.*

At the exact center of this whirling confluence of identities—G.N. Knapp and the author of the *Cantos,* presumed reader and imitator of Revelation—was Stuart, malignant presence in my cousin's life.

You don't want to find him, the counterwoman said, and now her grim warning took on a larger meaning: that he

had been, however he may have felt about Katy, a dominat-
ing and destructive influence; that to sustain domination, he
had resorted to more than harassment; that he had terror-
ized Katy; and that he was G.N. Knapp.

Down the Channel, a foghorn began its moaning admo-
nition. I turned off the lamp by my bed. At that moment it
struck me that, in all likelihood, Katy and I had not mentioned
wolves in our story: we knew that there had been no wolves in
the coastal regions of California since the last Ice Age.

Chapter 12

Before first light the next morning, over a rushed breakfast of undercooked oatmeal that burned my mouth, I studied my street map of San Francisco, but found no Wolf Street, Way, Drive, or Avenue to the west, where the dunes had been, or anywhere else in town. But I did find Point Lobos just north of Sutro Heights, Lobos Creek emptying into the Ocean at Baker Beach, and Point Lobos Avenue forking off of Geary Boulevard at 40th Avenue to the north and running out to the Great Highway. There was also Lobos Street in the Oceanview. Curious, I thought, all of them named after an animal extinct in the area throughout recorded history.

Without seeing the original version, I couldn't be sure, but as I remembered, we had set our story in the Nineteenth Century—the late Nineteenth Century, I was fairly certain—not in any specific year. Knapp had added the year 1873 to the story. Why? What was the significance of that year? Or was it a year? What if 1873 was an address, an invitation?

Wouldn't that be consistent with Knapp's sense of fun and with the story's weird hidden coherence?

By the time I got into my car, it was light. The City—or at least the western part of it—was fogged in and very cold. I drove Point Lobos Avenue from end to end searching without success for number 1873, then back to Geary. At 25th Avenue, I turned right and drove through the Park, through shadowy pines and black lakes in the mist, then south on 19th Avenue. Eventually, I found Lobos Street, just a few blocks long, old and new houses, most of them small and built close to the street with addresses from 1 to 300. The street was deserted, and the fog floated like a silvery veil over the tops of the huge, old, rough-barked Monterey pines along the edge of a playground, majestic remnants of a primeval woodland in a tough neighborhood.

Then, back to 19th Avenue and north again through the Park, then east on California and out Franklin.

In the near white-out, a tall, white building on Outer Broadway seemed to have come free of its foundation and to be adrift, its neighbors having nearly receded from view in the ground-level cloud mass.

In the suave elegance of the lobby, two sea deities lounged, one in each of the lower corners of a mural in muted blues and violets. They gazed across a scene of strange vacancy, a dreamlike San Francisco Bay without ships. And as in dreams, in which one can move without conscious volition from place to place, so the eye of the viewer drifted without satisfaction, rejecting the vacancy at the center of the scene, drawn to the figures at the periphery, then following their trancelike gaze back to the center, and so on.

The brass faced doors of the elevator opened and closed almost soundlessly. I got off at the top floor. Down the hall, I pushed a button set discreetly in the wall and waited. A woman in her seventies opened the door.

She wore a large marquis diamond on one hand and carved black jade set in gold on the other, a faded pink housecoat, and down-at-the-heel slippers. Even at that early hour, she had the rosy look of extreme good health that moderate obesity sometimes brings with it, regardless of age. She was shorter than I by several inches, but with her head tilted back, she always seemed to be looking down at me.

"Don't you have a watch?" she asked with affectionate garrulity.

"It's at home."

"What's the idea of bothering people?" my mother's old friend asked as she kissed my cheek and opened the door wide. "Don't disturb the neighbors." That was an old joke. There were none: her apartment took up the whole floor.

"What time is it?" I asked.

"As if you didn't know. Not even 8:00 yet!"

"You weren't asleep."

"So what? Come on. Of course, you haven't eaten."

She was wrong about that, but I didn't tell her. We passed the ghostly serenity of her living room, with its pale, silk-upholstered furniture, collection of museum-quality jade carvings, and Chinese water-colors from the Eighteenth and Nineteenth Centuries. On an ebony piano, tall, red chrysanthemums rose out of a spherical vase of heavy uncut crystal. A large window overlooked the Bay and hills to the north, though now in the fog, these could not be seen. We climbed a spiral staircase to a large penthouse room opening onto an equally large roof garden.

Beatrice Glass was having her breakfast.

"Would you like some?" She gestured towards a large white porcelain bowl containing pea soup with peanuts and Cheerios heaped on top.

She touched the wall, covered in gold tea-paper, pushed open an invisible cupboard, and took out a cup, saucer, and bowl for me.

"Consuela is off today," she explained while pouring coffee into the cup. "Another of her relatives has died." Then, sympathetically but also rather mechanically, she asked, as if of someone with a serious illness, "How is your father?"

"Fine, I think. Haven't seen him in awhile."

"Sorry about Edward, dear, and his daughter. Such a shame! She went to Los Angeles, didn't she?" That explained the untimely death.

I watched as Aunt Bea ladled out a large serving of pea soup in which floated, but could not be seen until now, slices of wiener.

When she reached for the "topping" of mixed cocktail nuts, I said, "Thanks, Aunt Bea, just soup."

We ate for a few minutes without conversation.

"Aunt Bea, were there ever wolves around here in the old days?"

Aunt Bea laughed. "The kind with four legs and a tail? Not that I ever heard of. Is that what brought you here so early? Aren't there books about things like that?"

"The library doesn't open until 10:00."

Aunt Bea watched me with unconcealed interest. "What's going on Bella?"

I ate my soup and did not immediately answer.

"How did your cousin die?"

God, she was sharp.

"I heard suicide."

I didn't answer.

"What about wolves?" She smiled kindly at me, and for a moment, I felt like crying.

"It's for something I'm working on. I'm trying to track down a reference in a short story about San Francisco."

"A scavenger hunt?" She looked hard at me over the intentionally misfired question.

"No."

"Nothing reckless?" she asked, meaning the opposite and ignoring my fabrication.

"Aunt Bea, I'm just looking for background. I found an old story, and in it is a reference to wolves at the beach. I didn't know there had been any, so I thought maybe I'd discovered a local legend or a native myth of some kind that I could develop. Anyway, I thought you might know something or other that would save me some time."

Some of it was true. One of my biggest sellers was based on an old story from the Hudson River Valley, and Beatrice Epstein Glass, the soap heiress, knew San Francisco and its history well.

"Ah." She ladled more soup into our bowls. "A new writing project!" She was not deceived.

"I've just started it."

"I see. What kind of reference was it?"

"Someone refers to 'the west, past the dunes. There are wolves.'"

"Lobos da mar."

"Wolves?"

"Sea lions."

"Sea lions?" I repeated, sounding stupid to myself.

"It's Portuguese."

"Huh! I was driving around this morning looking for Wolf Street." This was true, in a way.

"Bella, dear, in my day, only very *beautiful* girls got away with being dumb."

"Well I thought it might be the name of a street, like Wolf or Lobos."

"So. In a story, someone says that there are wolves around here somewhere. Are you sure you're looking for a street?"

"You mean Lobos Creek?" I asked. Aunt Bea's slightly open-mouthed smile made me feel like a monkey doing antic tricks. "It runs through the Presidio and out at Baker Beach. Is that what you mean?"

"I had a friend at school. Her name was Viola MacDougal, and she had a big nose. She was tall and gawky, and good at the piano. She married a conductor—I forget who—an Italian. They were Catholics."

She gazed into her soup bowl as though seeing in it the forgotten face. Aunt Bea smelled mischief. Retaliation would take the form of seeming irrelevancy.

"She was a lovely person, but homely. The conductor was a much better looking man than she was a woman. We wondered what he saw in her."

"Wealth?"

"No one could understand it! Viola's father had been extremely rich, but he lost everything in the Earthquake."

"How did that happen?"

"He made a fortune in—" she held her fire and watched my face—"flavored water."

A reaction was expected. I looked, and in fact was, perplexed.

"Nowadays, we have all sorts of things like that—sodas, flavored mineral waters, vitamin waters, and such. But Mr. MacDougal made money back then because his company had its own water source right here in town. He didn't have to pay to bring the water in, you see."

"Wasn't that why the conductor married Viola?"

Aunt Bea shook her head. "They *had* been rich, remember. But MacDougal took a beating because of the Earthquake. It really was a shame. There was a spring underground, you know, that ran from a source at the foot of what used to be called Black Mountain to Ocean Beach near Land's End. Supposedly, according to the Indian legends, anyway, there had once been many of these springs, but certain gods or animals—I forget which—sealed them away so that we humans could not use them. All but one, MacDougal's, which was said to have very pure water. But in 1906, it went away, like the others, dammed underground. There's a lake in that spot now."

"What did MacDougal do then?"

"Well, he was not, so everyone said, a man to give up. But I guess rebuilding the business with a new out-of-town water supply, and so on, was just too much for him. His wife went to work in a dress shop Downtown, and he drank. Not water."

"So why did the conductor marry Viola? Did you ever find out?"

"Looks aren't everything, dear," Aunt Bea said in betrayal of her original argument.

I threaded my way back through the story. "Aunt Bea?"

"Yes, dear?"

"What about the sea-lions?"

"Which ones?"

"The lobos da mar, remember?"

She looked at me with shrewd eyes.

"Lobos da Mar was the name of the spring, that's all."

Chapter 13

A wood-bound and tangled rose vine scraped against the weather-blackened shingles of my father's house. Everywhere were the sodden, brown remains of last summer's flowers. Roses, daylilies, and iris grew there each spring and summer in profusion that Roger Marx' indifference did not suppress. I climbed the flagstone steps leading to the house. A woman, slightly past middle age, wearing a flowered shirtwaist dress and Birkenstocks met me at the door.

"Well, Mrs. Silver!" She smiled in open-mouth expectancy. "We haven't seen much of you lately! Come inside. Oh dear. Your father's out. I'm so sorry. Were you expecting him to be here?"

I followed her inside. "No, Mrs. Sellers. I wasn't." I tried unsuccessfully to recall when I had last been there.

The spare and grudging furniture had never given comfort. Against the inexpensive wood paneling installed by my father was the couch he had made from a door topped by slip-covered foam rubber. The home-crafted tile and pebble mosaic coffee table was the gift of a colleague many years ago. A metal floor lamp of modern design and three canvas director's chairs completed the grouping.

"He's buying bait and so on for Friday's trip."

What good timing! My visit coincided with Roger's preparations for the excursion to the Dillon's house at Lake Tahoe, first weekend of the month since spring of 1957, men only.

"Would you like a cup of coffee? I was just going to have some."

"Thank you." I looked at my watch. The routine had not changed: coffee break every hour on the hour. No union contract would have taken Mrs. Sellers' needs so generously into account.

"It'll just be a minute," she said on her way to the kitchen from which emanated the familiar greasy smell of a half-hearted commitment to cleanliness. Except for this smell, the dark and quiet house seemed, as it always had, unlived in.

"Is there anything I can help you with?"

"Thanks, no," I said and without explanation, went into the garage and closed the door.

The house itself was unchanged over time, but the garage had become more crowded and disorderly. Cardboard boxes were stacked everywhere along the walls, in some places two or three deep and crammed with papers, books, magazines, records, tapes. There was scarcely space for my father's rusted Honda Civic. The sheer magnitude of the matter to be sifted through was daunting. I went back to the kitchen.

"Mrs. Sellers," I began, accepting a cup of pallid coffee, "do you have any idea what is in those boxes in the garage?"

Mrs. Sellers fluttered her eyelashes. The intended comedy of this mannerism had become ghastly with the passing of years. "The mystery of that garage is unfathomable to me," she said.

"I want to find some boxes that had my papers and things from college in them."

Mrs. Sellers sipped her coffee and slowly closed her eyes. In this way, she announced that she was about to say something regrettable.

"I *can* tell you about *those*, I'm afraid. They're not here."

"No?"

Mrs. Sellers shook her head with slow emphasis.

"You see, when Mister Marx passed on…" She waited for my acknowledgement, always making a point of referring to Katy's father as Mister Marx, as distinct from my father, who was Professor Marx. She cleared her throat before resuming.

"Some of the contents of the house in San Francisco were brought here." She took another sip. "You know only too well what the garage here has been. Well, something would have to go *out*, or the car, diminutive though it is, could not come *in*."

No room in the house for my things, of course. But I had no right to be resentful. I had my own house, much larger than this one, where I could store my souvenir rubble.

"In other words, my things aren't here anymore."

"I'm so afraid not."

"What happened to them?"

"Now, I take responsibility for this." She gave, as she had always been skilled at doing, the appearance of cringing, while actually communicating by indefinable means a nose thumb. "As there was simply no space in which to put a single, solitary, additional thing in that garage, I asked the Professor if I might clear some of the things out. He was returning home from lunch with Professor Dillon—" and here she left off with significance. Having imbibed, was understood. "He said that I might go ahead and do what was necessary."

It had always been wise to ask for things after lunch.

"What about Uncle Edward's house? Who sorted out the things over there?"

"Why, I did. There was no one else to do it. I think it was January. I packed the things that looked important, mostly financial documents, and disposed of the rest."

"What was the rest? How did you dispose of them?"

"Oh, just odds and ends. I couldn't say precisely. I carried them out to the street, which was very foolish, because of my back. You may recall that I injured it years ago and am not to lift anything of any size. But this load of boxes had to be put out for the scavengers, and there was no one else to do it." She sighed at the memory of the ordeal. "But do you know, now I think of it, the risk was taken in vain."

I assumed the usual meaning, that whatever Mrs. Sellers did was done in vain, since adequate appreciation was never shown. But this time there was another meaning.

"I had made, you see, an error. Trash pickup at Mister Marx' house is Thursday."

I waited.

"That was the day I did the cleaning-out. Had I but gone the day before, the gardener would have been there to assist me. As it was, the boxes and other refuse sat on the street for an entire week. The neighbors were very put out."

"Was there anything that looked like old college work—term papers, exams…"

"I don't recall off hand. I think so, but I couldn't be absolutely certain. I never thought they'd be wanted after so long a time," she said, slipping judiciously into the safety of the passive voice, the better to accuse by implication.

Anyone at any time that week could have picked up the story if it was in the junk thrown out. But also, whoever found it would have needed Katy's address, not to mention a reason for using it.

"And you only saved bank statements?"

"There might have been other things…"

"You know, Mrs. Sellers," I said, with an unconscionable forced smile of commiseration, "you ought to have shown a similar resolve with that mountain of junk in my father's garage. Aside from the inconvenience of having it there, it's a fire hazard."

Mrs. Sellers nodded in transcendent understanding. "This is true."

"It reminds me of the nests of those rats that keep everything, including their own waste."

Mrs. Sellers frowned.

"Well," I said, "the question is, where to begin."

Mrs. Sellers put down her cup. With a smile meant to signify a renewed appetite for work, she said, "And I must be getting back to my duties." Moving with unusual briskness out of the kitchen, she called out, "Do help yourself to more coffee!"

How Mrs. Sellers actually spent her time in my father's house I never knew. The house was not clean. In the kitchen, walls, cabinets, and appliances bore the condensate and dribblings of various vapors and fluids. Throughout the rest of the house, dust and grime covered all but the most prominently visible surfaces. It was less a conspicuous lack of cleanliness than a prevailing squalor kept just at the threshold of conscious perception.

I poured the remainder of my unpleasant coffee into the sink drain and walked to the garage. The Sybil had left me to enter alone the chamber where two ceiling bulbs provided scarcely enough light to prevent a drunken man from missing the door.

Chapter 14

By 5:30, against a deep blue evening sky, the megaliths of Downtown had lost their daylight look of indifferent brutality and taken on a shimmering, gilded beauty. But driving by them, heading west on the Bay Bridge, I scarcely noticed.

My father, who lived without close human attachments, was incapable of parting with any of the matter that came into his possession. Cardboard boxes stuffed with files, notebooks, magazines, records, books, audio tapes—all, to judge from their coatings of dust, ignored. If the story's there, if it's not there—so what? I suppose in a perverse way, it made me feel better to waste my afternoon in the atmosphere of unendurable futility of my father's house. Grief, loss, guilt—I could forget them for awhile and pretend to be doing something useful. Aliza's skepticism was reasonable, and, I knew viscerally, wrong. "The Hatchet Man" was not Katy's work, and it was not innocent.

I did not find "The Dead Do No Harm" that day, and as it turned out, I did not search through all of the boxes. I did, however, find something of interest.

I don't know how many boxes I dug through before I backed into a column of them and dislodged the uppermost four, including two bankers' boxes whose contents spilled out onto the garage floor. I restacked the two that had not come open because of being fastened with masking tape. Then I got down onto all fours and started gathering up the contents of the other two—bank statements and canceled checks—sweeping them together into an indiscriminate heap with the intention of putting them back in the boxes in no particular order. Inconsiderate, yes, but the boxes, the garage, the house all brought back associations and memories of a painful kind and a renewed and unwelcome sense of imprisonment in the past. But when I saw that these records had belonged to my Uncle Edward—not Roger—my irritation dissipated. I never had been angry with him, and now I was truly sorry to have made such a mess of his things.

The situation could have been a lot worse. These boxes must have been packed by someone in Edward's executor's office, with monthly statements wrapped around checks, some thick and fastened with rubber bands or paper clips, and some file folders which fell but did not spill their contents.

I don't know why I looked inside one of these. I never knew my uncle well. He always seemed, if not quite a god-like individual, a man whose ordered and decent life made him and his whole way of living in some way inaccessible to someone like me, barred as I was from it by my alcoholic and unhappy immediate family. Katy had problems, of course, but her parents and her home always seemed secure and safe in a way mine never did. Maybe opening his file was a way of entering their circle.

Inside were brokerage confirmation slips and a bank document on which the word annuity caught my attention. If Uncle Edward had created an annuity for Katy, what had she done with the money? I read through the document and discovered, to my amazement, that the beneficiary of this annuity was not Katy. His name was Gregor Kitteredge. I never had heard of him.

In November of 1966, my uncle placed over $3 million dollars in this annuity. The income was to be paid monthly for Gregor Kitteredge's lifetime, and on his death was to revert to Katy and, in the event of her demise, to his brother, Roger. I thought of Katy in Venice, alone, troubled, and poor, and for the first time in my life, was angry with my uncle.

Who was Gregor Kitteredge? Was I now to find out that my uncle was gay and Kitteredge was his lover? Or was Kitteredge Edward's illegitimate son—and Katy's brother? Was Kitteredge Knapp? Could the coincidence of initials be random? And if he was Knapp, why send the story, and why make those cryptic and menacing modifications? With his future financially secure, why pick on Katy? Was Kitteredge Stuart?

I restacked the boxes I'd knocked over and left.

Outside, I saw my father's car parked at the curb. Certainly, Mrs. Sellers had told him I was there, and it would have been awkward to leave without speaking to him. I found him in the back yard, where he sat reading in a lawn chair, the day's mail beside him on the leaf-strewn lawn. In one hand, he held a can of beer.

The setting was one of astounding beauty. The untended autumnal garden was its own realm, walled off from the surrounding world by trees and shrubs of which the aged and weathered shingles of the house seemed an organic extension. Leaves floated downward in clear, cold air, and the intense blue of the sky, seen through parting clouds, deepened in contrast to the clouds' brilliant white.

"Hello," I said as I approached him.

He turned only slightly in my direction. "Bella."

I gave his cheek an arid kiss, which he made no attempt to return, brushed dead leaves from the other lawn chair, and sat in it.

The garden's wild growth was varying shades of brown, except for the wine-colored leaves of the big Japanese maple at the back of the yard.

"How are you, Dad?"

"Better. And you?"

"Fine, thanks."

We sat in silence. I was in no hurry to explain the reason for my visit, which he knew by now, though he still would expect an explanation.

At last he looked up from *Modern Philology* and asked, "Read any good books lately?"

I took his meaning and smiled. "Nothing worth mentioning."

"I'm reading something good right now. It's so absorbing, so edifying, I can't put it down!" He yawned. "The reviews are especially worthwhile."

"Saves you reading the books," I said.

He drank from the can and dropped the journal onto the grass beside his real love. *Garden* had come in the mail that day, along with the Dutch Gardens catalogue of summer bulbs. If there was a mail order nursery that didn't have Roger Marx' name on its mailing list, it wasn't worth knowing about. He subscribed to all the glossiest garden magazines, regardless of their cost. But I had never seen him work in the garden.

He glanced at my clothes. "You're looking well, Bella. Elegantly dressed, I see. Book sales up?"

"I think so."

"I'm embarrassed to admit I still haven't read your work."

"Don't be. A lot of people are embarrassed if they have."

As if from nowhere, he produced a new beer can. He always had the knack for doing that. He popped open the top and drank.

"I understand that you had to confront the garage. That garage has become a chaos since your mother's time."

Ah yes. Mother's organizing ability. The attribute of a second rate intellect, of course, but an indispensable asset when put to the service of a gifted mind.

"Did you find what you were looking for?"

"No. I was trying to locate something I wrote in college."

He raised his eyebrows.

"For the *Daily Cal* short story contest."

"Interesting. Going to develop it for commercial purposes?"

"Possibly." The lie came from nowhere, like the beer can. I knew that his irony and contempt were only defensive, but that knowledge never gave me comfort.

"Would you like some refreshment?"

I shook my head. He wanted me to come to the point.

"I wonder, Dad, if you have ever heard of Gregor Kitteredge."

"Should I have?"

"Uncle Edward created a large annuity for him."

My father looked at me with distaste. "I can't pretend, Bella, not to be surprised at this unexpected and rather prurient display of interest in your uncle's personal affairs. Perhaps you ought to spend less time on popular fiction and give your mind more wholesome and nourishing food."

"Don't you really know about him, Dad?" I pursued, unable to stop, though inwardly daunted. "Over $3 million dollars. I wonder...did Katy inherit anything?"

He shook his head in disapproval.

"I wouldn't know. Nor is Edward's private life appropriate pasture for me, you, or anyone else to forage in. You do have other interests?"

I wanted to say, no. He seemed not to notice that I made no reply.

"I would have thought so."

He picked up *Garden* and placed it in his lap and in this way indicated that the interview would now end.

K. M. WOOD

On the other side of the bushes, children had been shrieking and laughing. Now one of them started to cry.

"What happened," came a woman's voice. "I told you not to go on that! Come inside right now!" A screen door banged.

I stood up.

Without taking his eyes from the magazine, my father said, "They're dead now, Katy and Edward. Let them alone."

He reached for the beer can and brought it to his lips. His hand shook with its old tremor.

To the air, he murmured, "Magnificent selection this year."

I looked down at the page on which blazed the crimson glory of a Hybrid Asiatic lily. Then, about to take my leave, I raised my glance to my father's face and was struck by its expression of unmistakable dislike. In another instant the look was gone. For a moment longer than usual, I let myself study the sagging face conspired against by dissipation and age.

"I'll be going now," I said lamely. "Sorry to have barged in."

I gave him another affectionless kiss, received one in return this time, and turning, walked out of the garden, along the side of the house, and out to the street.

Why had it never occurred to me that antipathy was mutual? Well, I had been wrong to think, as I always had done, that he had no feeling for me.

Chapter 15

When I left home the next morning, the display on my answering machine had a red nine on it. Two messages were from Aliza: the first, an innocent-sounding invitation to lunch that day; the second, a calmly delivered reiteration of the first and also, was I all right? There was a message from my publisher in New York about the proofs that had arrived for me the day before, or the day before that. I did not at this point care about them or the publisher. I was working on a different story. I did not listen to the other messages.

California is a magnet for dreams and those enthralled by them, drawn to the western littoral and barred only by the great Ocean itself from further relentless pursuit of whatever fabulous objective had summoned them. Here had come to rest the inventors of Hollywood, a second Venice, a castle made of bits of broken bottles and other litter. In the narrow confines of the western edge of San Francisco had once been a quarter-mile long swimming pool filled with unheated ocean water, an enormous glass and iron pleasure palace of seven swimming pools on wave-battered rocks, an amusement park, and a cliff with statuary positioned, in defiance of any rational principle, on its rough rock face. Mounted on the seawall separating Ocean Beach from the Great Highway is a sign that says, "Drownings occur due to heavy surf and severe undertow. Please remain safely on shore."

Across the Great Highway from where I stood, an eroded bluff covered in rust-colored ice plant rose steeply upward behind a low pink and blue wall that was partly buried in sandy soil. This was all that remained of Playland-At-the-Beach. A few yards to the south, where Point Lobos Avenue becomes the Great Highway, according to a 1901 Department of Public Works topographical map, Lobos da Mar Creek once flowed from its subterranean bed into the sea.

Time had completed the work of the Great Earthquake, though perhaps, to judge from a house at the top of the bluff, shored on the windward side, subterranean movement here was still under way. For among the possible causes of subsidence is an underground waterway flowing beneath a structure and augmenting whatever instability the underlying earth is subject to. I got back into my car, drove up to Sutro Heights, and parked.

The northern end of 48th Avenue starts at Point Lobos Avenue. A few blocks to the south, it curves sharply eastward into Sutro Heights Avenue, in this way avoiding the steep drop at the southern edge of the bluff. The house I'd seen from below was a large, gray stucco near the Sutro Heights corner.

Between Point Lobos and Sutro Heights, 48th Avenue has a mixed character. The east side is lined with stucco row houses built in the decade before World War II, costly now to a degree that would have shocked their builder and, no doubt, expensively furnished by affluent people for whom they had not been intended. The west side of the street is mostly occupied by Sutro Heights Park, the last remnant of Adolph Sutro's vanished estate, spread across the top of the bluff and overlooking the ocean. Adjacent to it is the gray house I'd seen from below.

From where I stood looking at its exposed north side, I could see what a large house it was—three stories, one of which, below street level, was glassed-in, like a greenhouse. The property was set off from the Park by a ramshackle wood fence, about six feet high, extending down slope from the house for about fifteen yards and enclosing an impenetrable looking forest of low juniper and other trees and shrubs. In the sandy soil of a small front yard, a scraggly boxwood border enclosed randomly planted succulents struggling for life and two large Monterey cypress trees that masked almost the entire front façade of the house. One upstairs window gaped, giving the place an untenanted look. The ancient bed of subterranean Lobos da Mar Creek was under my feet.

Only the thinnest filament of conjecture had led here, and yet I could not dismiss the idea that the site of the asylum in Knapp's version corresponded to a real place and that I had found it. What was I looking for? Would I recognize the person skilled in the malicious use of narrative and Biblical allusion? Venice was 400 miles away, and so was the man on whose physical strength a bus ride imposed severe hardship. Yet I felt his presence here and no longer questioned that "The Hatchet Man" was his work. I climbed the steps to the front door and rang the bell.

A woman in her forties opened the door. She wore jeans, a flannel shirt, and no make-up on an anxious face. Her brown, waving hair was held back on both sides by white plastic barrettes adorned with pink rabbit heads.

The entry hall was large and dark, paneled in gumwood with a broad stairway opposite the door.

"Good morning," I said, with an apologetic smile that was not entirely feigned. "I wonder if I might ask a very large favor."

"What's the matter?"

"I'm a writer. My name is Bella Silver, but I use the name Dyana Lynn Fairchild."

Her face told me I hadn't much time to come to the point.

"I write romantic novels—romances—and, you see, I'm working on a new novel now, and I saw this house. It really is just perfect—older and set on this bluff above the sea. Just exactly right." I had no plan, but an approximation of truth would serve my purpose. "I just spotted it from down on the Great Highway. I ought to have asked my publisher to send you a written request. But I wasn't thinking. I just saw the house and came right up."

"You want to see the house?"

"I would be very grateful to be able to see it. You see, atmosphere is so important in my books. I could come back, if there is a more convenient time." Who else was in this big, shored-up house?

"This is a private home." She closed the door.

Now, here was absolutely no tangible sign of any connection between this house and "The Hatchet Man," Stuart, or for that matter, anyone in my family. There was only a dark, unremarkable interior of the Craftsman Period and an unhappy looking woman understandably annoyed at a presumptuous request made by a stranger. What was I about here—using a name, my married name, that I rarely used and creating a fabrication to insinuate myself into the home of strangers?

But I wasn't capable of leaving, not then. I told myself that the irrational promptings are the ones to be heeded, because they lead to the deeper truths. I rang the bell a second time.

This time a different woman answered, like the other, middle-aged, in a plaid flannel shirt over jeans. Her straight, shoulder length blonde hair was tucked behind her ears and she wore rimless glasses and no make-up. Her smile told me that she knew how to deal with a nuisance.

"I didn't ask...Could I possibly make an appointment? I'll gladly make a gift to any charity you wish. I have a deadline. This would help me so much. Any charity you direct. Or possibly..." The idea had come suddenly. I held back, "Is it at all possible you have space to rent?"

"Mimi," came the other woman's voice from inside. "Mimi, can I speak to you?"

The woman in the doorway did not answer her.

"I can provide a reference from my publisher, Primavera Books. Perhaps, if this isn't a good time, I could buy you both lunch—tomorrow, perhaps. I know I'm a total stranger, and this is very awkward."

The other woman's voice was insistent. "If you don't mind, Mimi. I need to talk to you."

"Excuse me just a moment, the woman in the doorway said. "I won't be a minute," and she left the door ajar.

"But we *talked* about this," I heard the first woman complain. "We agreed on no more people. I thought we decided on just the eight."

"The room is just sitting there, empty. We don't use it. Besides, however many we have now, next month, who knows who'll be here and who won't, and we'll still have our payments. They don't change."

"Just the room, then, no meals."

There was a silence. Then Mimi said, "Think about it, Googe. We *need* the money."

Then the door opened again. "We do have some space upstairs."

In that moment, I was completely isolated, alone, without family or friends, belonging nowhere but here, facing this open doorway and unlooked for opportunity. I went in.

The entry hall gave onto a large sitting room furnished mostly with Victorian pieces of mediocre quality. The lamps and sofa were contemporary and inexpensive looking. At the rear of this room were double glass doors through which I could see bamboo furniture in a sunroom. Cushions covered in bright yellow plaid cotton contrasted decisively with the grays of sky and sea outside.

I climbed the maroon carpeted stairs with Mimi behind me.

There were five doors on the upper landing. One of these led to the common bathroom. Mimi pushed open one of the others, motioned me inside, and switched on the ceiling light.

The room was dowdy but welcoming. In it was a low, maple bedstead covered in white chenille, a dresser from the Golden Oak Period, a pine kitchen table to serve as a desk, and a braided rag rug covering most of a pine floor. An easy chair wearing what appeared to be a homemade slipcover of tan corduroy stood by a small table with a milk glass lamp on it. Two windows facing west looked out on the great expanse of ocean and sky.

"$600. There are other people in the house, including a little girl, but I would say it's a quiet house."

"Noise won't be a problem for me."

On the way to the stairs, I saw the bathroom. It was large and clean. The walls were painted in white enamel applied over unrepaired lesions in the previous coats. A plastic bottle of liquid hand soap stood on the sink. There were no personal toiletries.

As we went down the stairs, Mimi said, "Will you use the room just for working? We have a meal plan—an additional $300, you see. And kitchen privileges come with the room.

Except from 6:30 to 8:00 in the morning and 5:00 to 8:00 PM, which is when Gail prepares the meals—vegetarian. We have two refrigerators, one for house meals and one for individual storage. We each have a shelf in that one. I'll show you."

By now, we were back in the entry hall, and Mimi led me through a swinging door into the kitchen. The odor of burned fat and meat juices must have been inherited from the previous carnivorous owners, and the outspoken lemon yellow paint had been applied without scraping cabinet doors, so that they all stood slightly open.

Almost immediately, the other woman came into the kitchen from the dining room.

She poured coffee from a glass pot into a mug for me.

"I'm Mimi Gibson, by the way, and this is my partner, Gail Flahrty." Then, to her partner, she said, "This is Bella Silver, or what's your other name? (She's a writer.)"

"Dyana Lynn Fairchild." I showed them my driver's license and filled out an application, but gave my attorney's office address instead of my own.

The coffee was strong and well made. I drank it down and wrote a check for first and last months' rent and one month of the meal plan. Gail stood silently and unhappily by.

I placed my empty mug on the sink counter beside an unopened and new looking box of Tylenol, which was unremarkable enough, except that on top of the box was a small price tag bearing the name of a Los Angeles grocery chain, Ralph's.

I thanked the landladies for the coffee and for renting me the room and left. Outside, the morning had taken on that intense clarity that sometimes precedes and usually follows rain. The houses and green-black Monterey pines and cypresses, the hills to the north and south, Golden Gate Park, and the windmills stood out in exquisitely sharp detail.

Well, I had parted with $1,500 because of a vague trail of evidence leading to an old house whose connection to my cousin's death could scarcely be called even tenuous. Quite simply, I was no longer responsible for myself.

PART 3

Away

Chapter 16

The dining room was at the back of the house, and its windows looked out at the ocean. Now, their curtains were drawn against the blackness outside. They were seven at a round table, eating lentil soup of an unappealing gray-brown color. They transferred their attention to me when I came into the room.

Mimi said, "I'll do the honors. This," she nodded towards the elderly man next to her, "is Mr. Avery..."

"Phil," the old gentleman interrupted.

"Phil," Mimi conceded, "who lives two doors down from us."

"And Naomi Lewis, my former boss's daughter, who works at our branch library and lives right around the corner." Naomi was a young woman with curly, blonde hair framing a rosy and cheerful face.

"This is Lorne Cole, Sarah Taylor and her daughter, Solange, and Ann Nilsson. They're our other housemates." Ann appeared to be in her late sixties. Her silvered blonde hair hung in a long braid. She was dabbing with her napkin at some soup that had spilled onto her sweater and smiling in self-disparagement.

"And this is Bella, who is going to be writing a book in the deep freeze."

They all nodded and smiled at me, except for Solange, who was nine or ten years old.

"Hello, everyone," I said.

My original intention, of course, had not been to live in the house as a resident, but rather, to be there and to keep my eyes and ears open, to be an observer and in this way, to learn. But soon after arriving that morning, it became clear to me that I must not leave. What if I missed something—a word, gesture, or hidden object instantaneously glimpsed but leading to Stuart or Knapp? I had already seen something of interest: the Tylenol from the Los Angeles supermarket. Besides, once in my rented room, I found it a surprisingly hospitable work environment, so that my first day there was actually productive, resulting in an outline and synopsis for a new book.

Thoroughness is everything in scholarship. It can even compensate to some extent for intellectual dullness. The good scholar reads everything even remotely connected with the subject under examination and so, without fail, sooner or later, discovers the crumb on the forest path, and then another crumb, and so on, until stumbling on the truth sought. Someone in this group, and perhaps more than one person, had knowledge to impart.

I sat in the vacant place next to Phil, who was crumbling bread into his soup. He wore glasses with thick lenses, and wisps of his gray hair were combed across the bald top of his head. His teeth were irregular and discolored, but he had an engaging smile.

"Not too cold up there, we hope?" Mimi asked genially.

"No, not at all. It's very nice."

"We call that room the deep freeze, because it's the one furthest from the furnace, and the heating duct that serves it wasn't properly installed, so the room never seems to get warm enough, except on a sunny afternoon, which we did not have today. But the bed is good, and so is the view."

"The view is wonderful," I said. "So is the house. How many rooms are there?"

"Let's see," Mimi answered, "four bedrooms upstairs, and down here, the living room, sunroom—I don't think you've seen that yet—dining room, and kitchen. Ann has the room downstairs. That room was once a greenhouse. We still have a lot of work to do."

"Structural? I noticed the supports outside."

"Those supports have been up for years. The former owner said in the disclosure that the subsidence was caused by the excavation at the bottom of the hillside."

"Anybody here besides me remember Playland?" Phil asked.

No one had actually been there.

"Too bad," Phil said. "Ever had an It's It?"

There was a general shaking of heads.

"We'll, that's where they come from! V'nilla ice cream between two oatmeal cookies covered in chocolate. Invented at Playland. Now look at it. Gone. Nothing left of it at all. Tore everything down, and now there's just those so-called townhouses. Almost wrecked this place, too."

"Supposedly, there are a lot of subterranean streams all over San Francisco," I said. "Don't some of them empty into the ocean?"

Mimi took a drink of wine, and for no more than a second, looked at me with unusual interest. Then she said, "Lobos Creek lets out into Baker Beach. Do you know of any others, Ann?"

The older woman shook her head. "No, except that I believe Lake Merced was once the mouth of a wild river...before my time, of course!"

Mimi said, "Islais Creek that trickles down Glen Canyon used to be a river that flowed all the way to the Bay."

"A friend of mine had a photo of two men in a rowboat fishing in it," Phil said.

"Anyway," Mimi said, "this house, even with its minor structural problems, was a great buy. We were lucky to get it, and when it's all fixed up, the resale value will be a lot more than we paid."

From the kitchen came the loud thud of the refrigerator door being shut with some force.

"Expensive job," Phil said.

Mimi nodded. "We may be able to get the developer from down below to pay a good portion of the costs. If not, we still have a good investment."

I nodded agreement. "You know, I heard that one of the hills in the Inner Sunset consists entirely of garbage."

"There's a lot of fill—Downtown and the Marina—but fill isn't a problem if it's been properly compacted."

"The root, don't forget *it*," said Lorne, a young man with red hair and beard who seemed to be methodically getting drunk.

Mimi gave him a long look. Then to me, she said, "You see, there's an old story about a spring running right under us. That is, it would if it ever existed, and supposedly, growing directly above it, was a huge tree of some kind, and you can actually see what looks like part of the tap root that drew water from that spring."

"Is there a spring?" I asked.

No one answered.

Then Phil exclaimed, "Well, if they shut you down, that'd be just too bad!"

"Shut them down?" I asked him.

"For Heaven's sake, Phil! No one's going to shut us down. We're doing the repairs. No problem."

Phil explained, turning to me, "I'm a widower, you know, and I like a good, home-cooked meal." Then, to Mimi, "Delicious soup tonight. Potato peel broth—not a speck of meat—but so delicious!"

Gail, whose eyes were red-rimmed, brought in the next course, and for a while, no one seemed to have anything to say. We ate our vegetarian lasagna made with whole wheat pasta and fresh mushrooms, some of which had not been thoroughly cleaned. Salad came, too, and although the greens were of good quality and well washed and dried, the dressing was made with a blended, flavorless olive oil and an excess of raw garlic.

"By the way," Naomi said, "I've decided to take Ann's advice and do just what I want with my bedroom. It's going to be that plum color after all."

"Plum! Wonderful," Mimi said with enthusiasm, and everyone else nodded and smiled.

"Are librarians allowed to have plum boudoirs?" asked Lorne into his glass.

"I'm only an assistant librarian," Naomi answered without looking at him. Sarah looked disconsolately at her plate.

"They ever I.D. the fella they fished out of the water down below?" Phil asked. Then, politely to me, because I was new to the group, he went on to explain. "Stark naked! Been in the water a long time, real swollen, so there wasn't much left to go by." Then, he looked up from his plate. "Sorry folks! Not exactly table talk, I guess."

"What's table talk," Solange asked, glancing provocatively around the table.

"Conversation that is not about yucky things," Ann replied with a smile.

"Like?"

Turning to Lorne, Ann asked, "How's your mother?"

"Fine. For her."

"Lorne's mother isn't well," Mimi explained, turning to me.

"Yup," Lorne said, "that's what she's got, all right."

"Sarah has some interesting news," Naomi offered.

"What's that?" Phil asked putting down his fork. They all looked expectantly at Solange's mother.

"Oh, it's, well…"

Solange smirked.

With thin fingers, Sarah tucked her hair behind her ears and said, "It's just that I'll be covering the Outer Richmond Pottery Fair this weekend."

There was a general murmur of approval. "That's wonderful!" "Congratulations!" "Good work!" they all said.

Ann, who was sitting beside Sarah, patted her shoulder. "Good for you!" she said encouragingly. "It's about time, too."

Lorne glanced up at Naomi, but she ignored him.

"No more want ads, then?" Phil wanted to know.

"Oh, I'll still be doing them, but I'll also be doing this type of thing from time to time."

"Well, that's how you work your way into reporting!" he said.

"I hope so." Evidently, Sarah wasn't used to much attention, and it was making her uncomfortable. She kept her eyes on her plate, but went on talking. "Naomi," she asked, "our branch library isn't open on Saturdays, is it?"

"Not for the present, I'm afraid. Why?"

"I wanted to do some research—on ceramics—for the article. I want to write about the Fair from a historical standpoint."

"Why doesn't Lorne help you?" asked Solange with quiet malice.

The mother stared hard at the lettuce leaves soaking in oil on her plate and made an effort to smile as though she found her child's remark charming.

"Perhaps I could help," Naomi said kindly. "Of course, I'm not here all that much. But maybe Ann would help also. We could go over your notes with you after you've done some research. And I'll bet Mimi and Gail are both good readers, and that's all you need, really, a good reader."

They all looked at Phil.

"O' course! You can count on me," Phil said. "I'll see if I can find you some old photos of the Richmond. I still know people! You see…" he said, turning to me, but forgetting my name.

"Bella," Mimi prompted.

"Beautiful name," he said, adding with a wink, "no pun intended! I worked for a number of years in Otto's, prob'ly before your time, a fine camera store Downtown. 'Course, it's gone now. All the best photographers came in—the newspaper guys, all the pros. We knew 'em all. Otto was a real fat guy, and his brother was always in jail for something or other. But he took pictures, the brother did, of everything. He's the one might have some old pictures of the Richmond. If he's not dead."

"Would you ask him?" Sarah asked.

"Sure!" the old gentleman said. "I think I might know where to look for him, too," he added grimly.

"That'd be wonderful," Mimi said.

"You know, Sarah," Naomi said, "there's a whole series of books about American neighborhoods, with old photos. I've come across some about San Francisco in the catalogue."

For a while, they ate in silence.

"Anyway," Naomi said at last, "next month, we might be able to re-open on alternating Saturdays." She shook her head. "The allocations were announced last year. We're finally getting the funding."

"Government in action," Mimi said, holding up her wine glass before taking a drink.

Gail came into the room with a water pitcher and a look of cold fury for Mimi noted by Solange with a small, derisive smile.

The others moved on in conversation, pretending not to notice the emotions embarrassingly revealed, talking of the funding problems in the Library system, the unusual wetness of the season, due, it was agreed, to solar flares, the new produce market that had opened nearby, the second sighting of a nude man seen during the last rain at the beach.

"Bella, would you tell us about your book?" Naomi asked.

"Well, it's a novel."

"A novel!" Phil exclaimed. "Well, what's it about?"

I am not shy about the things I write, and I was about to give them a Dyana Lynn Fairburn synopsis—no problem remembering my plots—but Ann admonished them, though looking at me, "Sometimes, writers don't like to talk about their work, you know."

"My books are not great literature. They're just romantic stories. But I do try to give them atmosphere."

"We're a little out of the way here," Naomi said.

"Just what I wanted. This part of town is intriguing—the ocean, the hills and weather, all the trees, interesting history, and not a lot of people swarming all over everything."

"Except down the hill," Mimi said.

"But not up here."

Gail brought in little dishes of bread pudding in orange sauce and a pitcher of coffee. As before, the coffee was strong and well flavored.

"So," I began, turning to Mimi, "there's a librarian, and a—reporter. What does everyone else do?"

"Well, there are the ex-librarians—Gail, Ann, and me."

"You and Gail are retired?"

"That's sort of the way I think of us, though we're not retirement age. We both had jobs that really weren't what we wanted. We thought this kind of arrangement would give us a chance to find out what we wanted to do with our lives and also prepare for when we're older."

It looked as though Gail had already found out what she wanted to do.

Sarah, Phil, and Ann returned to the subject of writing about the Pottery Fair. Ann broke the skin of an orange at the stem and began to peel it. "But you won't need much help, Sarah," she was saying. "Your writing is good. How long will the article be?"

"Seven hundred and fifty words."

"I see," Ann said. "I wonder if you could find out about other pottery fairs in the area, or is the first one? What famous potters have lived here? Is there a prevailing style? Do you see what I mean?"

Sarah's eyes were wide.

"You just need to give yourself time for some reading, that's all." She poured coffee into Sarah's cup. "You'll do a wonderful job."

Sarah's eyes glistened. She looked about to cry. The older woman said, "This is a good beginning!"

"Try the San Francisco History Center at the Main Library," Naomi suggested.

Sarah nodded.

Ann said, "Have some fun with it!"

"Thanks, guys," Sarah said, and she actually looked more relaxed.

Gail began to clear away the dishes. Naomi and Phil said goodnight and went their separate ways. Lorne, who had been going his own separate way throughout the meal, did not say goodnight, but got up and left the house. Solange, without a word to anyone, left the table as though gnawed by hatred of a house with no television and no meat.

Chapter 17

I showered in the white bathroom and got into bed.

What was I looking for? A literary turn of mind, knowledge of San Francisco history or the New Testament? A religious zealot? Someone who knew my cousin. Someone who knew Stuart.

"Well, there are the ex-librarians—Gail, Ann, and me," Mimi had said, and librarians have the readiest access to vast amounts of information. Naomi and Ann, it seemed, had a fair idea of how to develop a piece of written work, and Naomi had pointed to Ann as especially capable of helping Sarah with the Pottery Fair piece. She had identified Mimi and Gail as good readers. Sure: they were librarians, so maybe they just liked books, or maybe they were experienced writers who knew how to manipulate language and nuance meaning, or both. Ann's advice to timid Sarah sounded as though it came from someone who had learned from personal experience as a writer and even perhaps as a teacher of writing. *Your writing is good*, Ann had said with some authority, and Naomi had offered to go over Sarah's notes.

Several of them seemed to have better than average knowledge of San Francisco history. Not everyone knows about the wild river delta that silted up and became Lake Merced or Islais Creek—two men in a rowboat, fishing. And then, there was the taproot, the old story about a spring under the house. Mimi and Lorne knew about that. Naomi was familiar with the Public Library system. Phil's access to San Francisco history was through photographers—*newspaper guys, all the pros*, including someone who took pictures of everything.

I could hear the soft boom of waves on the beach at the base of the bluff where the waters of Lobos da Mar Creek had emptied into the sea.

Ever had an It's It?

My mind was too busy with these people for sleep. Then, too, if Knapp was here, or someone acting with Stuart, that person might understand my reason for being in the house, and in that case, maybe I *shouldn't* sleep.

Around midnight, dinner began to exact its toll. I turned on the bed table lamp, pulled on my robe, and went across the darkened landing hall to the bathroom. Once inside, I could hear voices on the other side of the wall, Mimi and Gail in their bedroom.

"I could have gone back to work," I heard Gail say in a low, excited voice. "We didn't need them. It's just too much, and I can't stand it here anymore! You can't either—I can tell."

Mimi spoke next. I thought she must have been facing away from our common wall, because her words were indistinct. I lifted the toilet seat lid and sat down.

"I *can't* overlook it! He's a drunk and dirty, and she's so pathetic. And then the kid…"

Mimi's reply was unintelligible.

"Yeah, Naomi and Phil are nice, and the new woman seems OK, but that's not the point. We don't have a life."

Again, I heard Mimi's voice, followed by Gail's. "No. This is just no good. We tried it. It isn't working. At least it isn't for me. If it's so important to you to have a goddamn house full of people and a kid barging in wherever she feels like and rooting around in other people's things…"

Mimi must have shifted her ground, because now I heard her words distinctly.

"You mean the books. Yes, that was rather unfortunate. Solange is bored and unhappy. I don't particularly care for her either, but she *is* just a kid, after all, and those books— *The Wizard of Oz* and the others—*are* for children."

"Those are rare editions, and she left them on the floor with food lying all around." There was a pause. "Open, face down, spines up. Jesus! They could have been walked on, soiled—anything could have happened to them!"

"I'll put them downstairs in Ann's room. Solange doesn't go down to Ann's room unless Ann is there. I think we ought to move on, Gail."

"I see. So this puts the burden on me, again. As usual, you're passing the moral responsibility on to me. That's the way, isn't it? You're the nice one, right Mimi? You're always so reasonable." She was more excited now and getting loud. "Gail is the emotional one! Neurotic Gail!"

"Gail, the exhibitionist," Mimi rejoined quietly, so that I barely heard.

Gail heard well enough, though. "What a colossal jack off!" she shrieked.

There was a crash—something had been thrown—then a muffled cry, then a scraping sound as of a piece of heavy furniture being pushed against the wall, then quiet followed by sounds of evident reconciliation.

Farce is the comedy of rooms. It is almost inconceivable out of doors. One must have rooms for the machinery of farce to work: doors to open and close and walls for concealment. From the toilet, I saw the element of farce in my own present situation. But farce excludes the serious consequences of absurdity, mistakes of judgment, and lying. Real life is less benign.

What should I do? Leave the bathroom in silent stealth? Flush and leave normally? The toilet on this occasion—the dinner being what it was—must be flushed. At last, a course of action presented itself.

Quietly, I went back to my room, then immediately returned to the bathroom, closing the door somewhat more noisily than would have been considerate in a quiet house and turning the lock with a loud click. Then, I let the back of the toilet seat fall back against the tank. After an appropriate interval, the swoosh and gurgle of the flush sounded in the quiet. I washed my hands, and the cold water handle squeaked when I turned it. Then I unlocked and opened the door and turned out the light.

In the dark hallway, a thin bar of light from the slightly open door of my room fell across the floor and illuminated the bookcase and the pile of old books on the top shelf. I got back into bed, turned out the light, and waited. After a few minutes, I looked into the hall. It was dark. No light came from under any of the doors. The only sound was the wind rushing against the house. I went to the bookcase and carried the pile of books into my room.

These must be the books Sarah's daughter had used without asking—old editions of *The Golden Fairy Book* and *The Wind in the Willows,* among others. *The Wizard of Oz* had special meaning for me. It was a beautiful old edition with color plates. The illustrator was W.W. Denslow, so it had probably been printed around 1920, just before—as I remembered— J.R. Neill took over as illustrator of the Oz stories. I remembered Denslow's sign—the seahorse and abbreviated name, angularly printed on the illustrations—from the time when my mother read Oz books to me from editions like these, sitting, the two of us, without Roger and his judgments and alcoholic smell. I loved that strange, vividly colored world through which I had traveled in relative safety with my mother years ago.

I looked through several of the beautiful and well cared for books and admired the illustrations, some with pastel, others with jewel-like colors, all expressive and fascinating. Some of the inside covers bore the names of the original owners written in by hand or printed on bookplates. Some had inscriptions. "To Mary and Joan from Mother and Daddy, 1923" in a colorful Art Deco frame. Joseph R. Logan, Delta Nu House, Berkeley, 1904. This Book Belongs to Annie Goodman (*The Golden Fairy Book*, 1902). There was no date of publication on the title page of the small, handsome edition of *The Wind in the Willows*, but over the engraving of the river, with Rat standing in the boat and Mole at the oars, was an inscription in a child's cursive, and it made the hairs on the back of my neck stand up: "This book belongs to Julian Kitteredge."

Chapter 18

Two days ago, I had discovered a secret kept hidden in my family: the heir to my uncle's estate was a stranger whose family name now converged with the cryptic reference to wolves in "The Hatchet Man." It would appear that I had come to the right place.

But if the old edition of *The Wind in the Willows* belonged to Gail—say, if she was not Flahrty, but Kitteredge—what *was* her connection with the beneficiary of a $3 million dollar annuity—this near-slave to house she hated and in which everyone seemed to be short of funds? Was there a connection between Gail and the tertiary beneficiary of the annuity, my father, who would inherit in the event that Katy did not survive Gregor Kitteredge? And what was she to Stuart? I did not sleep that night.

When it was light, I washed in the white bathroom and went downstairs. The smell of coffee wafted up from the floor below.

The curtains were open, and I could see the ocean under a gray sky, the color of jade near the shore, darkening to slate further out to sea. A thermal pot of tea and one of coffee and two quart-sized cartons of orange juice were on the old fashioned walnut sideboard, along with a plate of bran muffins from which protruded black chunks of prune. Ann was sipping tea from a stoneware mug.

I took a muffin and poured some tea for myself.

"Good morning," I said, but Ann seemed not to hear. She was staring outside.

Just then, a gull swooped low a few yards from the house, a shot of white against gray that brought her back into the world of everyday life. She looked slightly startled for a moment and seemed not to recognize me immediately.

Gail appeared at the kitchen door. Her face was colorless and drawn. "Scrambled eggs or fried?" she asked.

"No eggs, thank you," I said, "but could I have a glass of milk, please?"

She withdrew into the kitchen without a word.

"A good day to stay in," I said.

Then Sarah came into the room. She wore a raincoat over a lightweight skirt and blouse that were not suited to the cold day. Her smile of greeting was strained, and her thin, white hands were unsteady as she poured her tea. She sat down beside me, and it seemed to me that this gave her comfort. She began to pick small chunks off of her muffin and eat them, but without any sign of enjoyment.

Gail brought in a glass of milk for me. "Where's Solange?"

"She isn't feeling well," Sarah explained.

"What's wrong?" Ann asked.

"Well, she had a fever last night. 102."

I wondered if Ann felt, as I did, that in a matter of seconds Sarah, who seemed struggling to control herself, would start to scream.

"Did you talk to the doctor?"

"I gave her Tylenol. That usually brings the fever down."

"But 102," Ann pursued, "wouldn't it be wise just to check in with the doctor?"

"Doctor?" The tone was sardonic. Lorne had come in. He took coffee from the sideboard, and went out again.

Pretending to ignore him, but now shaking perceptibly, Sarah said, "We don't have a regular doctor. Solange doesn't get sick very much. The few times she has, we've gone to the Emergency Room at UCSF. But 102 isn't that bad for a child."

She tried a smile, but the effort only set off a spasm of facial twitches.

"Is she better today?" Ann asked.

"Yes, the fever is down."

"She's staying home from school?"

"You're supposed to keep them home until they've been fever-free for twenty-four hours." Sarah's hair fell forward and screened her face. "I have to be at the paper."

"What's her temperature this morning?" Ann did not hide her uneasiness about the child who had been ill the night before and would now be on her own for the day.

"101.5."

A scavenger truck growled past the house.

Sarah put another piece of muffin about the size of a pea into her mouth. The effort of speaking and carrying out the little duties of ordinary social intercourse seemed an intolerable burden. She wiped her mouth, murmured something that sounded like "have a good day," and left.

Ann glanced at me, as though judging if I'd correctly observed what had happened. "Sarah is an hourly employee. She doesn't have paid time off, so she doesn't stay home when Solange is ill." She ate the remains of her muffin. "Did you sleep well?" she asked.

"Yes, thanks."

Gail came in with a second plate of muffins, put it on the sideboard, and began to clear the dishes from Sarah's place.

"You know," I said, "last night, in the hall, I noticed some wonderful old editions of children's books...*The Wizard of Oz* and some others."

Gail interrupted, "Mimi put them in your room this morning, Ann. I was worried about them up here."

"That's fine, Gail."

I ate some muffin. It had a gritty consistency and bitter taste—excess of whole-wheat flour, and oil had been added with a heavy hand to compensate for the drying effects of the flour. "I wish I still had my old books," I said. "They were given away." I felt Gail's angry stare. "I don't know why parents are always in such a hurry to get rid of things."

"More coffee, Ann?"

I saw a flicker of interest in Ann's eyes and guessed the reason for it. I was interested, too. I had not noticed that Gail was solicitous. Now, she was seeing to another's comfort and offering coffee when Ann was drinking tea.

Ann shook her head with a trace of the kindly irony I'd seen the night before and put up a hand to prevent the coffee from being poured, but she accidentally bumped the pot, and coffee spilled out.

Gail looked annoyed, but said as Ann started to rise, "Don't get up Ann. I'll get a sponge," and went into the kitchen.

"Not that one should dwell in the past," I said.

Ann's face showed resignation. I sympathized. I also hate conversation in the morning.

"I have friends who keep everything," I continued on this somewhat inconsiderate but necessary course, "their children's art projects and outgrown toys. They desperately hang on to something that isn't there anymore. Yet other people can't wait to give away anything that belongs to the past or reminds them of it."

Gail came back into the room with a sponge and wiped up the spill. Then she served herself a muffin, poured coffee into a mug, and sat at the table.

I said, "I think A. A. Milne said that *The Wind in the Willows* is a test of character. He said something like, 'We cannot criticize it, because it is criticizing us.'"

Gail was silent.

"How does it do that?" Ann asked.

"I'm not sure. The animals' candor and genuineness, perhaps. What do you think, Gail?"

"It was written for children," she said.

"It's full of death," I said.

Ann raised her eyebrows.

"It's about nothing lasting and mystery underlying everything," I went on. "And the idea of 'animal etiquette' that forbids any reference to danger or the disappearance of a particular animal. Death is accepted, but never talked about. But if it is never talked about, is it accepted?

"You see, the acceptance of death is a good thing. It's necessary. Life would be rather hard to endure if we couldn't accept death." This lesson I had learned.

"Well," I pursued, "I *don't* criticize. It's such a wonderful book, but why introduce the topic at all if it isn't to be discussed? Is this, after all, a suitable way to present death to children?"

"How *should* books present death to children, if indeed they should?" Ann asked.

"Well, probably not by emphasizing the subject or dwelling on it, but when they do bring it in, it ought to be in such a way as to help children come to terms with it by showing death not as the ultimate fact of life."

"Ah, now you are criticizing, I think," Ann admonished with a smile.

"Not at all. The book invites the question. Of course, there is a wonderfully healthy element in the book's treatment of death—a pagan element—nothing to do with retribution in the afterlife."

Gail pushed her chair back and went into the kitchen. The swinging door pumped air on my back.

I looked at Ann and saw that she was looking at me as my mother used to do, with a sad smile. I hadn't seen that look in a long time.

"Tell me, Bella, have you always been a writer, or have you done other kinds of work?"

"I was a teacher."

"What did you teach?"

"Literature."

"Will you ever go back to it?"

"No."

She frowned, and I thought I understood her unspoken objection. It was the general aimlessness of the time. People were adrift, searching for something or other, leaving what they most needed behind.

"My husband's death made it hard staying where I was," I explained.

"Ah," Ann said.

Gail could be heard washing breakfast things in the kitchen. She did not come back into the room while I was there.

Ann and I sipped our tea in silence that was not unfriendly.

"Interesting, you know," Ann said with a smile, "to find a younger person interested in antiquarian books."

"So Gail is a collector!"

"Gail loves old books and has a background in Library Science. But those books are mine."

I caught my breath.

No going back now. "There's nothing like reading from an early edition," I said. "It's as though one were reading in the author's own time. Although, sometimes, you know, reading the inscriptions in old books—like the one in that handsome *Wind in the Willows*—can be disturbing, an invasion of privacy, seeing things one shouldn't. I can't help wondering, for example, about the books' former owners."

Ann drank from her mug. Then she said—did I imagine, with an edge?—"Yes, I see your point. But I long ago learned to ignore the inscriptions and bookplates in the books I collected. The shopping was such fun. I remember an antiquarian bookshop in the Sunset. It was a dark, narrow little place owned by an old Armenian gentleman. I never saw him in natural light. He was so perfectly suited to the place. His skin was quite yellow, like old paper." It had been the merest glimmer of a change in her look, if a change it was.

"I remember that store," I said. "It was on Taraval. The old man dyed his hair black. There was a frayed, very nice armchair at the back of the store, and you could sit in it and read for as long as you wanted. That's where you bought the books?"

"I bought quite a few books there...and other places. Some I found at garage sales. I don't recall offhand which books came from where. At any rate, I would like you to feel free to enjoy my books whenever you like." She smiled at me.

Chapter 19

Olivia Beroni drove the black Jaguar XK convertible into the court-yard of her grandmother's Pacific Avenue house. It was a cold but sunny day early in December. The top was down, and Olivia had wrapped a wine colored cashmere muffler around her throat and heavy, dark hair. Reaching for the small Tiffany's gift box containing diamond and ruby earrings as a birthday gift for Grandmother, Olivia stepped out of the car. Tall and fashionably dressed, she stood for a moment looking out at the Bay and at the regatta in which, had it not been Grandmother's birthday, she would have been a participant in her own fast boat. But, much as she loved racing—the wind, the smell of the water, and the skyline of San Francisco seen from offshore—Grandmother, especially on her birthday, was far more important.

Since infancy, Olivia had grown up in her grandmother's loving and elegant home—since the time Olivia's mother had disappeared without a trace.

So began my new story, and, like "The Hatchet Man," it was a kind of lure.

"The books are mine." I could still hear the words and tried to digest what I had just learned. The Kitteredge book belonged to Ann. She had bought it in an antiquarian bookstore on Taraval Street. I wouldn't have tried to get away with a coincidence like that in any of my books.

Ann was lying, but why? The most likely reason was that she knew me. And if she knew me, hiding her connection with the Kitteredges, whoever they were, suggested an unpleasant depth of purpose. Was Stuart G.N. Knapp, or was she? G.N. Knapp, I'd assumed, was a pseudonym, and here in this house, now that I thought of it, there were alphabetic correspondences—G for Gail, N for what? K for Kitteredge. But N? Well, what about N for Nilsson?

I went for a walk, and left the Olivia Beroni file open.

The morning was cold with a sharp wind. Over the water to the north, another storm from the Arctic Circle was passing across the Marin Hills and absorbing their upper parts in its dark underside. The wind was from the northwest and made my eyes water. I turned onto Point Lobos Avenue and started down the hill towards the beach, passing Louis' perched above the sea-washed remnants of the Sutro Baths. A couple of tour buses were parked outside the Cliff House. As I approached the beach, I saw Solange sitting on the seawall facing west near the spot from which I had first caught sight of the gray house.

The sick child who should have been in bed gazed out at the blue-green sea and the rows of waves rolling in onto the beach. She wore a sweatshirt, cotton pants, and tennis shoes. The temperature with wind chill must have been in the forties.

"Hi," I said.

Solange looked up with a lack of expression and returned her gaze to the waves.

"See anything interesting out there?"

"What?"

"It's cold. Aren't you sick?"

There was no reply. I changed my course. "I was just wondering…Do you know where to get a good hamburger around here?"

The child studied my face with suspicion.

"Isn't there someplace?"

She watched me with narrowed eyes. "I don't know."

"OK. Thanks anyway."

"Why don't you eat back at the house?"

"The house? Oh, yes. Well, the food is very nice there, yes it is. It's quite good."

Solange smirked in disgust—at the thought of the food, at my lack of judgment, at the falseness of the claim.

"But I really feel like having a hamburger."

"Aren't you a *vegetarian*?" she demanded, the word ringing with contempt.

"No."

"Then why are you staying there—at Mimi and Gail's?"

"Do you have to be a vegetarian to stay there?"

She had not, evidently, considered this question. Her mouth opened in a babyish gape.

"I like the location."

Now, Solange was staring intently at me. Finally, she said, "Supposedly, they have good hamburgers up there." She pointed to Louis' up the hill.

"You mean that place?" I pointed at Louis'.

"I'll show you," she said grimly: adults never could do anything right.

"Great!" I said, as Solange climbed down from the wall, brushed sand from the seat of her pants, and started up the hill, walking fast and looking straight ahead as she led the way.

When we reached the café, I held the door open. "Care to join me? My treat."

The little girl looked up and down the street, then abruptly, she went inside, and I followed. There were red vinyl booths and white formica tables. A plate collection was displayed on the walls.

A waitress came to the table and without hesitation, Solange said, "Double Louis burger, medium, no onion. And a strawberry milkshake."

"Double burger," the waitress echoed approvingly as she wrote the order, "medium, hold the onions, strawberry shake."

I ordered an Original Louis burger, and when the waitress brought our orders, Solange fell on her double burger exploding with condiments with the voracity of a starved animal over fresh kill.

After some minutes without talk, I asked, "Are you a vegetarian, by the way?"

With a full mouth, Solange nodded. A look of aversion came over her face. Swallowing some, though not all of what was in her mouth, she explained, "See, no onions."

"Onions are vegetable," I said, puzzled.

"They go on hamburgers."

"I see. No onions, no questions."

The child smiled. It was the first time I'd seen her look pleased, but the look didn't last.

"Not that I get punished," she said glancing away. "Mother doesn't get mad." She shook her head and said, bitterly, "She gets disappointed."

My old wound ached, and for awhile we ate in silence.

"Where did you live before the house up there?"

"Berkeley. We had our own house, but we came here to be with *Lorne*."

"I grew up in Berkeley. Did you like Berkeley?"

I needn't have asked.

"My grampa lived with us. Then, we lived in our own house. It had a real back yard and a cherry tree. I had a cat."

I could imagine. They would not be going back. There was not to be another place like that. Now, there was only the dark house, the wind, and the twisted trees that turned black in the fog. "Could you get another cat here?"

"Lorne's allergic." She seemed gloomily to be puzzling something out. "They've all got something the matter with them. Mimi can't eat mustard. You have to be stupid to be allergic to that. Mother gets the hives if she eats chocolate. Gail's always mad."

Allergic to Mimi, I thought.

"I do have some pets, though. They're insects. I wanted to start an army, but I changed it to a hospital. I find sick bugs, and when they recover, I release them to the wild."

"Yes. Sounds interesting. And beneficial."

"I keep them in Ann's room. But even she hasn't seen my newest one, a flying bug with a red body—a Bark Beetle." She frowned. "It isn't really a Bark Beetle…or any kind of beetle. Its wings look like…you can almost see through them. A Bark Beetle's wings look like finger nails with red nail polish."

"Lacquer."

"Ann has the *Guide to Insects*, and the Bark Beetle was the only picture I found of a long red bug. It flew into my room. It wasn't really injured at all, but I thought I'd keep it just for a day. I wish I had a clear box. But even if I did, I couldn't move patients to it. They aren't strong enough, and in the brown box, Nonny might not find them."

"Who's Nonny?"

"A witch." Solange lowered her voice. "She lives in the house with us." She paused to observe the effect of this information. "She sneaks around and poisons the food. Not enough to kill you right away, but enough to make it taste really bad and make you sick."

I could vouch for this last part.

"Eventually, of course, you die. At night, after everybody goes to sleep, she puts spells on people. Sometimes she gets inside them, temporarily, and makes them act weird."

"How?"

"Well, Mimi and Gail—they act OK around Ann. They don't fight around her. But I hear them fight other times. Mimi and Gail. They both have a baby name! Mimi—that sounds like a baby name, and guess what Gail's nickname is…"

I just shook my head.

"Googie!" Solange said, revolted. "One time, Mimi tried to *kill* Gail."

"Really?"

"You don't believe me. It's true."

"What happened?"

"I couldn't see, but I heard them. They were in their room, and I heard yelling and a big, loud crash, and then Gail screamed! 'Go ahead and kill me!' That was what she said. I wish they would kill each other. They fight about money and Gail's job that she left at the *Survey*. If it was so great, why'd she leave it?"

"What kind of job?"

"I forget. Ann told me it had to do with measuring the earth."

"Was it the US Geological Survey?"

Ignoring my question, she said, "Must have been really great if she'd leave it for Mimi! Why doesn't she just go back?"

Good question. But what I wanted to know was, even if Gail knew from her work with geologists about Lobos da Mar Creek, even if she was Knapp, why would she hunt my cousin? My father was tertiary beneficiary of the annuity. No one else was named in the document that I saw. Had there been a more recent arrangement naming a different tertiary beneficiary? Were Gail and Ann in the hunt together?

"You know, Solange, when you're older, you can have a job and live the way you want to. You'll be able to have your own place and get a cat."

She studied the remains of the hamburger on her plate, as though trying to memorize the crumbs and the jewel-like brilliance of the drops of catsup and meat juices.

"I wish I could just live with Ann."

"She likes you, doesn't she?"

"Uh huh. It's nice when it's just her."

"When the others are away from the house?"

"Sometimes, Mimi and Gail go camping. Then, they take everything along. It takes them about ten thousand hours to load the car." In her own mind where her power was absolute, she need give no quarter to those she despised.

"Except last time. They didn't lug all their stupid crap last time, but so what?"

"Like what? Special camping gear?"

The child scoffed. "Sure. Their toast-R-oven. That's pretty special. And their generator. And all their clothes. And a stove and chairs! Why do they need them? The tent—well they need that, but it's so huge. Doesn't seem much like camping to me."

"With all that stuff, how often do they go?"

Solange shrugged. However often they went, it was not enough.

"I guess they don't go in much for camping in the colder months."

"They just *went*…for the colors," she added contemptuously.

"Well, some of the trees in the Sierras are beautiful in the fall. I'll bet they were caught in the rain."

"Yeah. I was, too. I went trick-or-treating by myself, but I wasn't allowed to stay out very long."

"What did you go as?"

"A ghoul. Ann gave me an old jacket and a scarf, and I had sunglasses and fake fangs."

"Sounds good."

"And then, when I went to bed, I didn't have to hear Mimi and Gail fighting. They were gone for two whole nights."

"They took all their things for just two nights?"

Grudgingly, Solange admitted, "Not this time."

"Maybe they didn't go camping."

"That's just where they go."

Unless they had business somewhere else—Los Angeles, for example.

"Don't they ever visit friends or go skiing?"

"They don't like anyone but each other, and they can't ski."

"So you only had peace and quiet the one weekend."

"No, they went other times. Anyway, they didn't take Nonny along last time. I know because I saw her Downtown." She watched my response. "You don't believe me, do you? You think I made Nonny up! But she's real. Listen." Solange leaned closer to me and lowered her voice. "My birthday is October 16, and this year Mimi and Gail gave me money. I wanted some *Force 2* comics, so I went Downtown to this special comic store by the train station. I'm not supposed to have them. They're *violent*. So when I got the money, I went Downtown on the bus, and I saw her."

"Nonny?"

Solange reached into her pocket and withdrew a toy Luger, which she placed on the table.

"That looks dangerous," I said.

"It's just a toy."

I pictured the child asleep with the Luger under her pillow in case Nonny should pay her a visit.

It was a female house whose dark, withholding, and barren genius had become embedded in the child's imagination in the person of a witch who hung out around the Amtrak Station on 4th Street.

The waitress brought a pot of tea for me and a slice of cherry pie for Solange, whose appetite the big meal had not sated.

"She goes out of town for orgies."

"Oh?"

"To avoid detection. And she takes the train. I *saw* her!"

"At an orgy?"

She closed her eyes, appalled by the stupidity of this question. "*Leaving* for one. She was going into the train station, and she had a suitcase with wheels on it, and she was walking right into the station." With a glance at the Luger, she said, "You can't tell witches just by looking at them."

That much was true.

"That house is haunted," Solange observed, but to herself, rather than to me. "Something is the matter with everybody there."

"Not you…"

"Not Ann, either."

"Not me," I said. "Are you still hungry?"

Solange hesitated before nodding. Whether or not she was still hungry, she wanted more to eat: when would such an opportunity come again?

"We could share something," I suggested. "How about ice cream?"

"A hot fudge sundae."

I caught the waitress' eye and ordered.

"What's the matter with Ann's friend?"

"Cancer, like Lorne's mother. Lorne's mother lives in Fort Bragg, and sometimes he goes there."

"Who takes care of her?"

"I don't know. No one, I guess. We might move there."

I didn't need to ask how she felt about this possibility.

"I was just starting to like school here. Lorne's mother is probably as crabby and mean as Lorne."

"Maybe now that your mom's job is changing, she won't want to move."

Solange shrugged. She was not reassured.

"Do you get to do anything special when you and your mom have the house to yourselves?" It was an unkind question, to which—and because—I already knew the answer, but it had another purpose.

"Sometimes Ann and I play Fish or Concentration. She taught me Cribbage, too."

"Ann seems nice."

Solange nodded. "Mother tried to get Lorne to let her go to Fort Bragg with him." The look of disgust that I'd seen before darkened her face. "I almost got to stay with Ann."

The sundae came, and Solange went to work with the same energy as before.

"Didn't they go?"

"No. Ann had to go see Mary. That's why I went trick or treating by myself. She's the only one who'd go with me."

"Mary's the sick friend?"

"She lives in Orinda. It's near Berkeley." It seemed as though even the thought of Orinda, near Berkeley, filled Solange with nostalgia. She licked fudge sauce from her upper lip and stood up. The corners of her mouth were still painted with white and brown remnants of her treat. The ice cream dish was empty.

"Thanks," she said, looking sorrowfully around the room.

"Let's go back to the house and get a jacket for you," I suggested, putting on my coat. But when I looked up, she was gone.

Through the window, I saw her trudging down the hill on her way back, I supposed, to sit in the wind and cold on the seawall. Now that the treat was finished, the normal conditions of her life, having been temporarily rescinded, were once more to be endured.

I paid for the lunch and walked outside. The ocean had turned from blue-green to celadon gray-green under dark clouds. The waves' white foam rushed over the rocks below where I stood overlooking what remained of the Sutro Baths, its plunges and other offered pleasures now reduced to a low, barnacle-encrusted ruin.

Not including Nonny, the witch, there were five travelers in the house. I had a fair idea—and it gave me no pleasure—which of them had spent time in LA.

Chapter 20

I walked back up the hill, but did not return that morning to my rented room. Tomorrow, Saturday, was the day of the Outer Richmond Pottery Fair, and with any luck, I would have some time alone in the house. For now, I thought of Stuart.

A #38 Geary bus sat at the corner of 48th and Point Lobos Avenues. I climbed on board just as the driver started the engine. The only other passengers were a middle-aged couple speaking German to each other. At 36th Avenue, we could see Downtown in the distance to the east, a miniscule etching against a white sky. I got off at 26th and walked north to my house.

Blanca, my cleaning lady, had been in my apartment the previous day and had left it immaculate and arranged according to her own exacting standard of order, which did not permit papers and odd items to be left lying visible in a living room. The papers, of course, had been placed in a neat stack on the desk in my bedroom at the top of which lay Stuart's pouch.

I pulled out the clipping, black blot on one side, fragment of map on the other showing the area around a city called Cimcit, "ibu" on what could have been a masthead line. At the bottom of the map, somewhat to the southwest, an arrow pointed to an incomplete name: hkent. What was it about this pouch, or its contents, that could cause such a violent, spasmodic reaction in Stuart—the convulsive coughing and bloodied sleeve, the horribly inflamed face and eyes, the fight to breathe?

I hauled the Atlas from its shelf in the living room and found Cimcit. It is in Uzbekistan, about a hundred miles north of Tashkent.

The San Francisco Main Library has a newspaper collection, as I had recently been reminded, and so has San Francisco State. But I went to Berkeley, to the basement of the Doe Library and the Newspaper Room.

Behind the service desk, a short, middle aged woman with a Buster Brown haircut was whispering excitedly to an unresponsive young man with the head and demeanor of an Athenian sculpture.

"And in the second place," she hissed, "where was he trained?" She waited.

The student assistant turned to me.

"Where are the *Oakland Tribunes*?"

"Before or after 1955?"

"Well, that's the problem," I said. "I'm trying to trace this clipping." I presented the scrap.

He looked at the stain, then at the map on the reverse side. "Not much to go on," he said dubiously.

I pointed to the arrow indicating Tashkent. "Maybe the State Library Index would give us a date on whatever happened in Tashkent to make international news."

The young man turned to the computer terminal on the service counter, turned the monitor screen so that I could see it, and typed. In a few seconds, the message came up: "Tashkent, USSR, destroyed by earthquake, April 25, 1966."

"*Tribunes* after 1955 are in the second aisle from the end, back of the room," he said. "Over there is the subject index for periodicals." He pointed to a microfiche reader near the door.

I thanked him, and the woman with the Buster Brown resumed her monologue as though there had been no interruption.

I found the *Oakland Tribune* volume for April 1966. The *Tribune* carried the news from Tashkent on the front page for three consecutive days and on page eight for one more day. All four were accompanied by maps of descending sizes, all of them larger than the one in the pouch.

I closed the book and went to the Index Table to check the entries listed under Tashkent. The *Tribune* had actually run five stories on the earthquake in Tashkent: the four in

April, starting with the day after the quake, and another, November 1, reporting a powerful aftershock on October 31. The story on the aftershock was also accompanied by a map of the Tashkent region. Stuart's pouch with the clipping in it was in my pocket. I took it out. It was an exact match with the one printed with the aftershock story. But on the reverse side of the page was a full-page ad for a Capwell's sale. The text that had been blacked out on Stuart's clipping was "GREAT BUYS ON EVERY..." in block letters.

Why on earth black that out? Was this another of Knapp's playful devices, or Stuart's—phantoms gliding past and through each other, in one moment indistinguishable, in another gliding apart? I'd paid little attention when the sick man said that he hadn't "lost them all." Something else—other clippings?—had been in the pouch, but now were gone.

I walked back to the stacks, found the *Berkeley Gazettes*, and took down November 1966. On page three of the Saturday, November 1 edition, I found the story. The headline read, "Tashkent Killer Aftershock," and here, I was more fortunate. On the reverse side of the aftershock story was a piece of local news. It was a short one-paragraph account of a hit-and-run accident in the Berkeley Hills the previous night. Names of the victims were "withheld pending notification of next-of-kin."

I turned to the next issue. It was Monday, November 2, 1966. Now I remembered. The *Berkeley Gazette* had published only Monday through Saturday and not on Sunday. Reopening the *Tribune* volume, I turned to Sunday, November 1, and there, at the end of Section B, was a story about the hit-and-run accident in the Berkeley Hills. It had occurred on a Friday night, Victims' names were not released until after the Saturday *Gazette* went to print. But Sunday's *Tribune* published the names.

BERKELEY HILLS HIT-AND-RUN INJURES 3

Late Friday night, a hit-and-run motorist struck a parked car on Northhampton Avenue seriously injuring a family of 3. UC graduate student Julian M. Kitteredge, 28, his wife, Graceann, 29, and son, Gregor, 4, were taken to Herrick Memorial Hospital with severe injuries. Parents' conditions were listed as serious. Gregor Kitteredge's condition is listed as critical.

Tucked away among the minor disasters and private tragedies of other people, knit together with these on the page of an old newspaper, was a malignant fact about my own family. The enormity of my uncle's guilt, concealed for decades, was only suggested by the consumption of his entire estate owing to Gregor Kitteredge and his injuries.

I took the volumes to the Xerox machine and made copies of both stories.

"I was simply pointing out that certain things are not meant for repetition—that when I made that comment, it was not for general circulation. And furthermore, I was quoted completely out of context!"

Her handsome assistant, as before, showed no interest in her remarks.

"That was so cathartic! You should have seen her face! Of course, I don't expect anything to change. Not with her being so territorial and, as we know, emotionally needy. Did I ever tell you what she said to Don at the last staff meeting?"

The sibilant harangue trailed me down the hall as far as the stairway. On the main floor I stopped to look outside. The bare, black branches of the cherry tree near the east entry shivered stiffly in the wind. Then the familiar face of a man, slim and elegant in a cable knit sweater and gabardine trousers, passed without noticing me and disappeared into the stairwell. I followed him upstairs and into the gracious old Reference Hall lined with oak cases above which tall windows showed the windblown treetops outside and stretched to the lofty ceiling.

Without turning to see who approached, he seemed to feel himself pursued and turned to face me.

"Joel," I said, catching up with him at last.

He regarded me blankly at me through thick glasses that magnified his eyes. Then his face broke into a smile of recognition. "Bella! Well!"

"Hi," I said and took the hand he held out. It was soft and slim, but held mine firmly.

"Slumming?"

"That's right. How's everything?"

"Couldn't be better. I have something coming out."

"Again? You just published last year. The Tudor bestiaries—I loved that!"

"You read it?" He was delighted.

"Of course."

His pale, almost transparent skin reddened with pleasure.

"And your work?" he asked.

I suddenly felt a spasm of embarrassment over my current career as a writer of romantic drivel. "I haven't taught in a couple of years now."

"Ah. I'm sorry. I'd forgotten," he said gently.

"Joel, I want to ask you something." I hung back for a moment, knowing he would be disappointed when he heard the sort of question it was. "It's about...It's not a scholarly question. You see, I'm trying to find someone. The name is Kitteredge. Might have been faculty."

"What's the matter, Bella?" I had approached him thoughtlessly.

"I don't like to bother you with this, Joel, but it's kind of important."

"What's the name again?"

"Kitteredge. Julian Kitteredge."

There was no point in trying to conceal anything from him. He looked gravely at me—though, as always, kindly—and he knew something was wrong.

He took my arm. "Come on," he said and led me back into the Main Loan Room.

"Where are we going?"

"I don't even know if he's here today," was the oblique answer. "He had a heart attack a couple of months ago, and I haven't seen him around. We'll see."

He ushered me through a leather-upholstered door into the Catalogue Room where a fat, bald-headed man in shirt sleeves sat writing. I had heard of him. This was Lipnauer of Catalogues.

"Josef, I'd like you to meet a friend of mine," was Joel's pleasant address. "This is Bella Marx, formerly of the English Department."

Lipnauer's bushy eyebrows rose in acknowledgement of the introduction. He spread his arms and rested his hands magisterially on the sides of his desk, pushed out his jaw, and regarded me, augustly, in silence. But my friend's airy approach bypassed Lipnauer's imperiousness. "Bella is trying to locate someone, an old friend. It seemed best to come to you."

I now saw in Joel a previously unrecognized subtlety. The flattery was in what had been left out, and it was a form of flattery to which the other man was clearly susceptible.

"Why don't you consult the University Directory?" Lipnauer asked.

"Yes, of course. But Bella feels that the person in question may no longer be here. Was, but no longer is." He turned to me. "How long ago?"

I hesitated. "Twenty or thirty years?"

"Well," said Lipnauer, as if to say, "You should have consulted me sooner."

"What name?"

"Kitteredge. Julian Kitteredge."

"Do NOT reshelve!" he growled at a woman who, cowed, replaced a volume on the reading table.

Lipnauer watched the woman's back as she retreated into the stacks. "Kitteredge." He grunted. The process of retrieval seemed to be underway. "What area of specialization?" he asked.

"I don't know," I answered uncomfortably.

"History of Printing and Bookbinding in California," he murmured complaisantly. "Yes. Very capable. Published, too, I think. That was in Tillotson's day. He hired a number of good people."

"Julian Kitteredge was a librarian?"

"Julian? Did you say Julian? Goodness, no. Graceann Kitteredge was on staff. Back when I first started here. What ever happened to her?"

"That's what I'd like to find out."

"Was she a friend of yours?"

"Of my family's."

"I see."

"We would like to find her."

"Indeed. Well, I can't be much help, I'm afraid. As I recall, now that I think of it, she left rather suddenly. For what reason I do not remember, though I must have known at the time." He frowned, and his forehead seemed about to collapse onto the lower part of his face. "Have you been trying to locate her all this while?"

"Not until recently."

Joel looked at his watch and broke in with an apologetic smile, "Awfully good of you to give us your time, Josef."

Lipnauer gave Joel a stern, almost suspicious look, but Joel seemed determined to avoid awkward questions. "By the way," he said, "I hear you're finally getting some help in here."

Lipnauer's expression changed. He closed his eyes. "I have begged them for years to give me someone—anyone! The work in here is too much for one person. I pleaded with them. Then I had my attack. Now, they see!"

"I should think so!" Joel commiserated. "Management problems are chronic around here, I'm afraid. At any rate, we mustn't take up too much of your time, Josef. Thank you."

Joel took my arm, and we turned to leave.

"Thank you, Mr. Lipnauer," I said, digesting the lesson to be learned from the ease with which I was making up my phantom life as I went along: perhaps I spent too much time *planning* my books and ought to try a more spontaneous approach to narrative development.

I said goodbye to my friend, knowing that his mind was uneasy on account of my visit. Should I have told him the truth?

Maybe. I could have presented my errand in a more rational way and explained its purpose: "I'd like to find someone named Kitteredge. I found some old family documents, and think that there might be some family connection with this person..." Joel would probably not have worried about me had I done that. And yet I liked him too much to lie. The facts might have been accurate, but the presentation would have been dishonest. This was not a matter of disinterested curiosity about a family event unknown to me until recently. Curiosity was altogether the wrong word. I was now driven by fervid compulsion that was a kind of emotional avarice.

Outside, the sun had gone into the clouds. A sharp, cold wind blew, and dead leaves floated in the air and onto the pavement. I saw that it was 2:40 by the Campanile clock and remembered, for some reason, when the Plexiglas barrier was installed to enclose the viewing platform at the top of the tower, and my father explained that its purpose was to deter suicides during final exams.

Chapter 21

Phil and Naomi were not at dinner that evening, and the tensions in the house were painfully apparent. Sarah and Lorne sat in glum silence. Solange, now with a sore throat, cough, and fever hovering around 103, was given her dinner in bed. Mimi and Gail did not speak to each other. The main dish was spanikopita oozing a clear, green fluid.

"Bella," said Ann, "may I ask you something about yourself?" This was a statement rather than a question and a declaration of severance from the emotional bleakness of the room. The adroitness of strategy was awesome, a ruse used as a ruse.

"Yes, certainly." I wondered if I had permanently lost the capacity to address a question on only one level.

"You are a writer."

"Technically, yes."

She smiled and looked puzzled.

"You're humble about your work."

"Well, it's a commercial product."

"I have always wanted to write a novel," she said. The others looked at her. "It would be about self-imposed unhappiness. The protagonist would be...old, self-pitying, and resentful. He dislikes his wife, but depends on her completely. She is like a useful and necessary piece of furniture. When, at last, she dies...what do you think?"

"He realizes how much he loved her?" Mimi proposed.

Ann gave her a smile of friendly remonstrance that I found chilling. "He positively exults! He wishes she had died sooner and freed him from dependence and from the crippling burden of her company. Then, he begins to remember her, and his memories are different from what the reader saw during her life. Now, we see her as having been full of subtle cruelty."

"How will it end?" I asked.

"Don't know," she said with a laugh. "Haven't started it yet."

She raised her fork in the air, leaned her head slightly back, and gazed at the small piece of onion impaled on it. Did she, like me, object to undercooked onion?

"The difficulty," she went on, "would be to avoid preaching."

"True," Mimi said.

"Still, it would be nice to save souls," Ann pursued good-naturedly.

"Yes, I agree," I said. "But that kind of thing is hard on a story."

"Have you written many novels, Bella?"

"Well, I guess I could say I've written one, but in several different versions. What about you? I thought last night when you offered to help Sarah that you might also be a writer."

"Ah, no."

No one spoke for a while.

Then I said, "I'm having a bit of trouble with a new element I've decided to add."

Gail came into the room and I waited for her to sit down before I went on. "I'm going to work in a murder this time. Usually, of course, I write about love. But to tell you the truth, I need a change. The atmosphere here makes me want to branch out, so to speak. So this story is going to be told from the point of view of a murderer who has committed a crime—for love, of course—and has not been caught and has to live with the consequences of the act. I don't know yet whether my publisher will go for this—departure—especially since the murderer is a woman."

Mimi was studying my face. "You know, Bella," she said ruminatively, "I think I've seen you before. I thought so yesterday, as well."

"I don't remember our having met before," I said. "Where do you think it was?"

"I don't know," Mimi said, looking puzzled. "Anyway, what's wrong with having a woman murderer? What's the matter, Ann?"

Ann seemed to be looking for something in her trouser pockets. "Forgot my pill," she said. "Be right back."

"Are they downstairs? I can get them," Mimi offered, but Ann shook her head and went out.

"Well," I explained, "in our genre, women can be strong up to a point, but it's the men who do the real work. It's old fashioned and sexist, I know, but you'd be surprised how many really devoted readers there are of this kind of fiction. If I make the victim really repellant, so that even the reader wants to see her go, maybe I can get away with this plot."

Ann came back into the room. "You're making yourself sound a bit criminal," she joked.

Gail frowned and went into the kitchen. She came back with one large and one small bowl of salad. The small bowl was for Mimi. The rest of us served ourselves from the large one.

I speared an unruly piece of romaine leaf. The corrosive dressing with its sting of raw garlic, excessive vinegar, and pepper heat made me want to spit the stuff into my napkin. But I swallowed it down, feeling community with the others, all of us navigating between the rock of the horrid salad dressing and the whirlpool of Gail's displeasure should we openly rebel against eating the terrible food. I looked round the table and saw them all in suspended animation, as if inwardly pondering this dilemma. Each person reacted in a way that seemed typical of his or her nature. Sarah looked despairing. Addressing this challenge was far beyond her slender resources. Lorne simply left the table, apparently having reached the conclusion that the well-being of the inside of his mouth was more important than Gail's good will.

Ann, with her good manners and subtlety, had found her own polite solution. "Well," she said cheerfully, "I'm bushed. It's time for bed and hot milk. When you're old, you're old. Goodnight, everyone." She folded her napkin, placed it on the table, and went out.

Mimi was on the point of saying something, or was she? Her face wore a look of bewilderment which, in seconds, became absolute horror. Her eyes bulged, and her mouth opened wide showing her tongue, red and glistening, drawn back into the depths of her throat from which came strangled cries and gasps. These continued as her hands curled into claws and worked frantically at her throat.

The firemen arrived just minutes after Gail dialed 911. There were three of them, but only two came into the house. One carried an oxygen tank. They seemed to fill the dining room with a robust and selfless competence alien to the house. Then, paramedics arrived, injected Mimi, and took her away. Gail climbed dismally into the back of the ambulance.

Chapter 22

Dear Mimi,

I am going.

I used to like my life. I liked my job, and taking the bus home evenings and walking up 19th Street to the white Queen Anne, changing from office clothes, and making dinner, vegetables and cheese. A book was all the company I needed.

It was a quiet, satisfying life. Companionship was something one was thought to need, but I was happy by myself. Then, when we were getting to know each other, our friendship was an enrichment, at least at first, until your life began to absorb mine. How did it happen? When did it begin?

Buying the house seemed like a reasonable thing to do, because paying rent was, as we said, throwing money away, and since we were spending so much time together, it seemed like a good idea to go partners in an investment. But from the moment we signed the papers and deposit checks, the friendship began to deteriorate. The house began consuming us—or, at least, me. Now I am in a trap and all I feel is anger.

As God knows, I was not conscious of what I was doing last night. I have always taken the greatest care with our food and always used the greatest caution in separating your food from any other. Your salad was always placed on a separate dish and never served from the main bowl. To prevent any possibility of dressing your salad from the wrong bottle, I always replaced other people's dressing, which sometimes contained mustard, in the refrigerator before pouring your dressing—without mustard—onto your salad, always.

But last night, your salad had mustard in it. If help had not arrived when it did, you would have died. This cannot have been accidental. Although my act was unconscious, it must also have been intentional.

I am sorry that I have hated the tenants. My problems are not their fault. I chose for myself. I gave up privacy and freedom in exchange for servitude.

I liked my old job at the Survey. It was a compromise after graduating with honors, but the projects were interesting, and the people I worked for were intelligent, and they appreciated me. Best of all, I didn't have to live where I worked. I'll try to get something like that again. I'm now prepared to lose the money I put into the house, because I'm leaving.

I am sorry.

Gail

The letter was lying open on the dining room table when I went downstairs to breakfast the next morning, and I read it.

Coffee and tea urns, corn muffins, and orange juice were on the sideboard, as before. But there was silence in the kitchen. I was alone in the room. The house now seemed pervaded by the deep gloom that resulted from a prolonged illness or death.

Gail could have had access to specialized information about coastal geology. Her first initial matched Knapp's, and even though she had manners enough to apologize for trying to kill Mimi, she was, according to her own assessment, a dangerous person. But I no longer suspected her of being G.N. Knapp. It was Ann who was connected with my family. Ann could have heard about Lobos da Mar Creek from Gail, or Mimi. Like Gail, she was occasionally out of town. I could imagine Katy liking Ann and having some sort of rapport or friendship with her, but not with Gail. Everyone liked Ann.

I was not hungry and did not want the food, as I supposed, left out by Gail before she took leave of the house. But I put a muffin on a plate, poured tea, and waited. It was Saturday, the day of the Outer Richmond Pottery Fair. Solange, coughing, was first to leave. A horn honked in front of the house, and she ran out. Sarah left soon afterwards in brown leather boots with worn heels and a peasant skirt longer than her raincoat. Following her out was Lorne, wearing reflector lens sunglasses for which there seemed no need that sunless morning. I wondered how and why he was involved with Sarah, who seemed to revolt him. I hadn't seen Ann that morning.

I ate the muffin, drank the tea, and went into the kitchen to put the plate and mug in the sink. Through the window I could see, some three or four yards away in the house next door, an elderly Chinese woman in a smock and jade earrings. She was cleaning her kitchen sink, her attention absorbed in the task. She rinsed the sink, and disappeared without noticing me. I went back through the dining room and up the stairs, which protested with soft creaks as our stairs at home had also done and mocked Roger's slow, determined ascent.

At the landing, the bedroom doors stood open, as usual, for ventilation of the rooms: mine, Mimi's and Gail's, Lorne's and Sarah's, and next to it, a sunroom that was Solange's. These two rooms were a littered confusion of unmade beds and jumbled clothes. Solange's room with its many windows was cold. Except for the stuffed Winnie the Pooh, nothing in it suggested that a child lived there.

Next door was the room Mimi had shared with Gail. I walked in, and for an unpleasant moment, I felt what Mimi was almost certainly to feel, coming back alone to the deserted room. It was in perfect order. On the large Victorian oak dresser were a mille-fleur bowl, a hand-blown indigo bud vase, a basket filled with dried flowers, a framed photo of a bridal couple taken, so it appeared, in the 1950s, and a snapshot of Mimi sitting on a couch between an elderly man and woman. The bed on its brass bedstead was neatly made. A plaid blanket was folded at the foot. In a corner near the window was a white wicker chaise lounge beside a low bookshelf made of particle board and painted white to match the walls: Virginia Woolf's *Diary*, *Tess of the D'Urbervilles*, Anaïs Nin's *Diary*, a series of *Sunset* do-it-yourself books, a book of

Diane Arbus reproductions. Against the window was a large desk of Scandinavian design, made of birch or some other light colored wood, a laptop, and a ladder back chair, and on the floor, a multi-colored braided rag rug. The white home-made curtains were open.

An old house makes noises, creaks and groans caused by wind and molecules expanding and contracting in response to temperature changes. Now, with the wind blowing hard outside, tree branches scraped against the house and windows rattled. Among these various sounds, I heard the closing of the front door.

I froze and listened. Again, only the wind and rattling noises. Nothing else from below. But someone was down there.

I went into my room and made a floorboard grunt under my feet. I left my door ajar and sat at the desk. My file was open, and I tried to look as though I'd been working.

A moment later, someone was on the stairs, coming up slowly. When I looked into the hall, I saw Lorne's hand as he closed the door to his and Sarah's room.

Chapter 23

When would he leave again, and when he did, how much time would I have in Ann's room before someone came home? I had not heard Ann go out, but the wind could have masked the sounds of the front door closing and her footsteps on the stairs outside.

I was too overwrought to work. I lay on the bed and waited for Lorne to leave for what turned out to be the better part of that day. At last, at about 4:30, he went out again. The sun had dropped under the clouds and cast a dark gold light on the water near the horizon. The others would surely be coming back soon.

Downstairs, I opened the door leading to Ann's part of the house and called to her. She did not answer. I went down. The door at the bottom of the stairway was fitted with a key-operated deadbolt. I knocked, and there was no answer. I knocked again. There was always the excuse of borrowing a book, as Ann had invited me to do.

The door was unlocked. I pushed it open and stood for a moment, surprised at the beauty of the place that was like the unfixed locus in a fairy tale or dream. The room was suffused with the deepening rose-bronze glow of the sunset. The west and north walls of this former greenhouse were made almost entirely of glass panes, as was the door leading outside to the garden, accessible by a half dozen or so wooden stairs. The garden itself was overgrown, as I had seen from the street on my first visit, with bushes and junipers whose tops extended from the house like a rough, dark green carpet in the air.

Facing west was a single bed furnished all in white with a gauze skirt, a large, fat pillow in an embroidered case, and a thick down quilt. Beside it was a small marble-topped occasional table on which were a handsome steel task lamp and a spider plant in a white porcelain cachepot. In one corner near the bed, a door led to a compact and bright, though windowless, bathroom with an African violet in full bloom on the toilet tank.

Along the west-facing glass wall was a fine, old oak dining table serving as a desk, a small ceramic heater in one corner, a grape ivy plant erupting from its white ceramic pot beside a yellow hand-blown glass candlestick and candle, and a porcelain cow under whose udders tiny yellow and blue flowers grew in the grass. There was also a brown shoebox with a punctured lid: the insect hospital.

Next to the desk facing diagonally into the room was a large easy chair upholstered in white canvas and a brass floor lamp. Mounted on the south wall were two shelves. Here were the old editions, some of which I had already seen and admired, twenty or thirty in all. The floor was cement and was almost completely covered by a sand-colored Berber area rug.

I took down *The Land of Oz* and then *The Boy's King Arthur* with N.C. Wyeth illustrations. I had a good idea what was inside. Sure enough, in their front covers was inscribed "This book belongs to Julian Kitteredge." In *Robin Hood* was "To our dear Julian, Merry Christmas with love, Uncle Lionel and Aunt Ruth, 1946."

The closet was beside the door leading upstairs. At first, I thought it was locked, because the knob refused to turn, but it was only an ornamental knob. I pulled, the door opened, and I stood looking into the closet. So it seemed at first. In fact, this was an unfinished cellar extending back to the hillside on which, barely discernible in the lightless interior, cement had been poured to prevent soil slippage.

In the recesses of this subterranean space were six large cardboard boxes neatly stacked, and just inside the door was a dresser painted white. On it was a small bowl containing potpourri, a flashlight, and a carefully polished silver frame, containing photos. It seemed odd that photos would be in a closet, that is until, looking up close, I saw Uncle Edward in tennis whites beside my father in his fishing clothes, Lake Tahoe and the Nevada mountains in the background; Uncle Edward and Aunt Vivian in front of their home with Pudgy and Duke; and Katy at the wheel of her Mercedes-Benz. Then I heard the front door close.

Chapter 24

I looked for a way out, but there was none. The garden door was also fitted with a keyed deadbolt. The stairs were carpeted. The only sound was the wind rushing past and the low trees outside whose branches scratched at the walls.

Ann closed the door, turned the key in the lock, and put the key in her pocket. At first she seemed not to notice me. Then she looked my way and smiled.

"Oh, dear. I hope I haven't startled you." I said.

Ann was not startled.

"Not to worry," she said and lowered herself into her comfortable upholstered chair. Her gaze moved from my face to the books in my arms and back again.

She sighed deeply. "That's better. I did a lot of walking today. I went to the Pottery Fair, of course, and walked part of the way home. I'm bushed," she said, and looked it.

She nodded towards the door to the stairs. "Oh that. Force of habit, you know. I usually lock it when nobody else is in the house."

Why not today? Had she been expecting a visitor?

"I'll be moving soon," she went on. "The stairs are not a good idea for me, you see. Such a nice room, though. Just not very practical for an older person."

Very reasonable, all of it. The door remained locked.

Had she realized that my presence in the house was not accidental? How could she have? Only my married name was on my driver's license and, for that matter, on the residence application which she could have seen lying about somewhere, like Gail's letter. And as for looks, Katy and I looked more like our mothers than like each other, except for our hair.

"I took you up on your offer about the books. Maybe I should have waited 'till you got home, but I had a bad work day, and that means a bad day all around."

"That's perfectly OK. Would you like to sit down? It's dreary upstairs. Things seem to have imploded."

I sat at the desk. "How is Mimi?"

"She's with her brother and his family in the Peninsula. The hospital wouldn't keep her, and she's still weak. Her brother came up and got her. And you had a bad day."

She still made no move to unlock the door.

"I shouldn't complain," I said. "I've done quite a few of these formula projects. The basic elements of plot are in place, and besides, they're pretty much always the same. But fleshing the story out can be hard. The more you have done it, the harder it gets, because you don't want to be repetitious: readers would be alienated. But then, because of the kind of fiction it is—commercial, after all—you feel guilty about having trouble with it."

"Was that the problem today?" She smoothed her skirt, and the momentary look on her face reminded me of yesterday's breakfast conversation and her sympathetic but weary resignation to unwanted talk.

"Today I tried something new." I was fleshing out a new plot at that very moment, or more accurately, an old plot.

"Something new...What's bad about that?"

"The plot is too intricate."

"Well, plenty of good books have intricate plots."

"Would you like to hear the story?"

"If it would be of help."

I had the feeling that she knew part of it already.

"You won't feel obliged to like it? Well," I began, "there is always the same heroine. She is beautiful and wealthy, and in my books, there is something in her past that she does not know about."

Ann nodded. She was again looking at the books in my lap.

"Olivia Beroni is the name of my current beautiful and wealthy person. Exotic and elegant in appearance, she is a world-class orientalist and director of acquisitions at the Museum of Far East Asian Art. Olivia was raised by her wealthy and eccentric paternal grandmother, an Italian countess, in a large house on outer Pacific Avenue with an unobstructed view to the north. Why was she raised by her grandmother?"

Ann shook her head. She gave me an encouraging smile.

"Olivia's mother disappeared immediately after Olivia's birth and was never found. Her father died on the Bay in a boating accident when Olivia was very little. All of her life, Olivia wanted to know about her mother and find her.

"One day, a letter written in Chinese arrives at the Museum addressed to Olivia, who is fluent in several Asian languages and often receives such mail in the course of her work. But when she reads this letter, she rushes to her car: the Lung jades may be bequeathed to the Museum. Olivia drives to an address near the westernmost end of the City, Seacliff. The house overlooks the ocean and is surrounded by huge cypress trees.

"A young Chinese woman admits Olivia into a gorgeous interior lavishly furnished with Chinese art, porcelains, and silks. Intricately carved ebony screens inlaid with mother-of-pearl shut out the daylight. The famous collector Eric Norman is also in the room. He is handsome and wealthy and has a reputation for ruthlessness.

"Olivia does not at first notice a gaunt old lady in a yellow coat of silk brocade that is a work of art in its own right. The old lady greets Olivia in Mandarin, in which Eric Norman is also fluent, and explains that she does not expect to live long and wishes to leave her collection to the Museum. Mrs. Lung asks Olivia to return the next day with the Museum's attorney. Eric Norman wishes to buy the jades and has already made an offer.

"The next day, when Olivia returns with the attorney, the two are met by the Lung butler who tells them that Mrs. Lung is unwell and wishes their appointment postponed. But from what the visitors can see of the entry hall and living room, the furnishings and artworks are gone."

"Eric Norman?" Ann put in but then answered her own question, though to herself, not to me. "No, that would be too obvious."

"Yes. This is like a game." True in more than one way. "You have to apply the formula, but each time in a new narrative. The hard thing about writing formula fiction is that if you depart from the model too much for a more truthful approach, your readers will be unhappy."

"But the truth can sometimes be fantastic. So far, I haven't heard anything that sounds untruthful or false."

"You will—if I tell you the rest of the story. That night, Olivia returns to the house and climbs inside through an unlocked window. She has a flashlight and walks through the house finding room after room denuded of furnishings. Then, she returns home and finds Eric Norman waiting for her. He tells her that Mrs. Lung has disappeared. He thinks that she has come to harm and tells Olivia that she may also be in danger, as he saw someone following her as she drove away from the Lung house."

"But is he—Norman—reliable?"

"Ah. We shouldn't think so at first. We should suspect his motives, as Olivia does. But he will show, later, that he is genuinely concerned for her safety.

"Then, he tells Olivia the story of the Lungs. Mrs. Lung's late husband, many years older than his wife, was a merchant who brought his young wife to San Francisco in the 1930s and amassed great wealth. The Lungs had only one child, a daughter. Norman asks Olivia if she knows why Mrs. Lung decided to give her collection to the Museum when he had offered a high price for the collection and agreed to leave it to the Museum at his death. Why had Mrs. Lung declined his very attractive offer? He notices Olivia's ring, a dragon carved in black jade, the stone traditionally symbolizing rage."

"A family saga," Ann said to the window and the dusk falling outside. The sun was down, now, and a fierce red glow spread above the horizon and across the water.

At that point, not even I, telling the tale, knew the full truth of her assessment. "Yes, and it is also about accidents with evil consequences. Olivia will discover her ancestry.

"The Lungs' daughter went to medical school and then, in her first year of residency, she was involved in a terrible accident. This was a crime of negligence which resulted in the death of an innocent person."

"Medical negligence?"

"No. Moral negligence. You see, one night, Mai Lung attends a dinner party in the Berkeley Hills. Driving home on a curving stretch of unlit street, she comes upon three people getting into their car—a man, woman, and little child. Out of nowhere, it seems, comes Mai in her father's car, a dark blue Cadillac. She is driving too fast. There is a collision. In an instant, the lives of the three people in the family—and Mai's life as well—are changed forever. The child is seriously injured. The parents become haunted by their responsibility for what happened to their son."

Ann was frowning down at her hands, folded her hands in her lap. "*Their* responsibility? What about the driver of the car?"

"Well, she is the first cause, of course. And here is where the untruths come in. She panics and drives away. She is not drunk, mind you, only going too fast on an unfamiliar road. She hits the parked car at about the same moment she saw it, then drives back to San Francisco, parks her father's car Downtown, and makes the rest of the trip home by cab. After all her hard work and achievement, the prospect of a ruined career leads her to make a criminal choice, and this she does not reverse, ever."

"And how does all of this relate to Olivia?"

"Olivia's father died soon after her mother disappeared, and Olivia was raised by his mother, her paternal grandmother. But Olivia will discover that she is also Mrs. Lung's granddaughter and Mai's daughter. You see, Mai marries and has a child, but soon after starts to have problems. Mental problems. She becomes addicted to medications which she prescribes for herself and is eventually institutionalized, but escapes and disappears."

Still not looking at me, Ann asked, "But what is the problem you're having?"

"My readers expect a happy ending. But they also want justice to be done, at least poetic justice, according to which the medical resident with a brilliant career ahead of her would have to suffer consequences. Then, too, a happy ending, or something close to it, isn't necessarily at odds with real life.

Crimes are not always punished. In real life, she might get on with her life. And would we all be better off with absolute justice performed and a criminal punished or with one more physician in the world to relieve human suffering?"

Ann sighed.

"I hope I haven't tired you."

"Not at all," she said to the darkening outside. "Your story is quite engrossing. How did you come up with it?"

"I invented most of it, except for the hit-and-run accident, which I got from a newspaper clipping someone gave me."

"Ah," she said quietly. "You began with fact, and then created an entire *world* from the possibilities lurking in an actual event."

Now, we were getting somewhere.

"Lurking," I repeated. "I never thought of it—the process—in quite that way." All at once I had the curious sensation of never having enjoyed a conversation so much. The bottom was not there. That was how it felt pushing off down a black diamond hill.

"That's always the way, actually, although the distance between the narrative and actuality varies. For instance, I can write about something that happened to me. I can render it exactly or embellish or alter the event to suit my purpose. I can write about something that happened to someone else. Or I can write about something I've only imagined but that could have grown out of a real event."

Ann was silent.

"Thank you for hearing me out," I said. "You really have helped me. My problem hasn't been with the story at all, but with myself. I see now that I haven't really focused on the characters. I need to invent biographies for them, for example. That is what Virginia Woolf did." This wasn't only Woolf's technique.

"Even for minor characters. Even for characters who only figure in the story by reference, like the victim-family. What about their lives before the accident? I need to work all of that out. Where did they come from? Was the mother a sophisticated New Yorker or a fundamentalist Christian, or—say—from the somewhere in the Heartland."

It was too dark now to see her face. It was all shadows. The wind tore at the house.

"That wind—our storms here, in fact—they're nothing. Little puffs to someone from the Midwest. 'Why,' that person would say, 'back home, we had *storms*. Real storms that turned the sky black! Not just gray, but black! Cyclones like the end of the world, and in winter, snow almost to the roof, and blizzards you can't see in!'

"From what I know," I pursued, "apocalyptic nature is a fact of seasonal life in the Midwest. It is the heart of normalcy in America, where there is even a town called Normal!

"And maybe this Midwestern young woman was ready to leave home for, let's say, California—Berkeley—the University. And that is where she met her husband. I would make him younger than she—a renowned scientist, because no one is average in romance fiction—and obsessed with his work, always in a hurry. Hence, the accident."

A good guess, evidently. The probe had hit the injured place. Ann turned towards me with a look of appraisal as though seeing me for the very first time. But then the kindly smile was back, only now it seemed to me like a mask, and this it must always have been.

"But he did not cause the accident."

"A disaster can have more than one cause," I said.

"They were married," she murmured. "Then they had a son and thought of having another, but not right away. They loved this one too much."

We were no longer discussing writing.

"One night," I said, picking up the narrative from her, "one night the family met with grief, an accident, a Cadillac on a narrow, dark, winding road."

"A Cadillac?"

"The type of car was not my choice. You see, in the actual event, the car was a Cadillac. A dark blue Fleetwood." Neither newspaper article had mentioned the type of car suspected in the accident. But Edward had such a car in those days.

"Do you know," Ann said, "I remember reading about an accident like that years ago, a hit-and-run in the Berkeley Hills, like the one in your story. Only the accident I'm thinking of was a little different. For one thing, the car was not a Cadillac."

Chapter 25

We sat in the unlit room. Darkness had fallen outside, and the rain began again, barely audible in the wind, at first just a faint spattering against the windows.

"There was a good deal of talk about this—tragedy—at the time, as I recall. The little boy was badly injured. With proper care, he might be able to walk, in time, but his brain was damaged, and he would not develop normally—would not really develop mentally, at all. He went to a facility."

"This all happened long ago," I said, watching her hands in the shadows as they began again the skirt-smoothing.

"Yes, but these were University people, so there was a lot of talk."

This might have been just a tale for a stormy night. But it was Ann's own story, I knew.

"The boy's father committed suicide, and the son, when he was about to turn 21, had a massive seizure and died."

"How awful," I said and meant it. The little torn fragment of news clipping on the reverse side of the Tashkent disaster was coming to life, rising from its long obscurity in this dark room.

"Yes," Ann said.

"One day that same year, the mother received a letter. It was from a bank. Not so unusual, you might say," she said with a nod towards me and a smile, "except that someone else's name was above the mother's address on the envelope and in the salutation line: it was the name of a complete stranger—a *Mr. Edward Marx*—and the name of his law firm, and for some reason, her own deceased son was mentioned in the letter. Some sort of data management error."

I felt at the edges of this story, told in the third person, but with little attempt now to disguise its personal character. I had entered a different and alien universe, one in which this stranger had, in a manner of speaking, collided with my uncle.

"There had been an annuity, so the letter said, and her son had been the beneficiary. The mother had never asked about the philanthropic fund that had supported her son's expensive care. Payments had gone directly to the facility. What was this about an annuity?

"Mr. Edward Marx' office was on California Street, and she went there, but only to learn that he had died. She found his address and went to look—just look—at his house. It was a large house—very comfortable looking."

Yes, this was true. The house had a wonderful solidity and was full of light and warmth—so different from my parents' house.

"When I saw the letter," she said, no longer pretending, "I began to think about the philanthropic fund. It had supported Gregor's care in an excellent facility that my husband and I could never have afforded. But what if that had come from some other source? What if that source was Mr. Edward Marx? What if *he* was our benefactor? What if he, Mr. Edward Marx, was the driver of the Death Car?"

She thought for a moment. "Of course, I was grateful. What would have happened to Gregor if not for that money?" And after another pause, "But what would have happened to all of us if not for Mr. Edward Marx?"

"How do you know he was the driver," I asked, but she went on without answering.

"I looked back on my life. Other people had done things. Other people had taken responsibility for themselves. They had *acted*. I never had, not really. I had always *adapted*. Always managed with whatever there was. But not anymore. Things had been out of balance for a long time, a very long, very bad time, and there was a debt to be settled. Now," she said grimly, "it *could* be settled. Now, I was to take responsibility. I was in control. Unfortunately, though, the person who, more than any other, had changed my life, the person who had destroyed everything: that person was...no longer available. But there was someone else, someone close to him, who was. A proxy.

"Mr. Edward Marx had a daughter, and I found her, my benefactor's child."

She needed to tell the story as much as I needed to hear it, but she was no longer talking to me. She had retreated to a place of her own. Her face was turned towards the storm outside, but she was looking inward.

"Ms. Marx lived in Venice. Venice, California, that is. And as luck would have it, a job opened up at UCLA, and I took it. I rented a place in Santa Monica and went to Venice and met her. We became friends. And there she was, living on the beach. Gregor had lived most of his life in confinement with one third of his brain functioning and lucky to have a day without a seizure.

"On the beach, she and I became acquaintances, then friends. And my new friend, it seemed, had had problems and was starting over. I went often to Venice to see her. She was working on a project. It had to do with Alfred Hitchcock—a project of great complexity. It was the center of her life. Actually, it was more than that. It was a source of nourishment and comfort. It was a kind of life raft. And for me, she herself became all of these things.

"I shared her interest in movies! What is more, it was in my power to *help*. As UCLA Library staff, I had access to the wonderful Film School collection, and I began reading a great deal in the literature about Hitchcock. It is important as we grow older to develop new interests and take up new activities. That is what I did. I gave her information about recent works on Hitchcock, at least at first, and there was always something new—articles in every kind of journal and books. One must stay abreast."

The plan was well designed. It would have been torture for Katy, this litany of ever more new sources to consult and her own merciless indictments of her work, especially when compared to that of others already in print.

"But," Ann continued with a smile, "the information that I gave her seemed to cause distress. How well I understood. If you have ever worked on an ambitious project, you know how very demoralizing it can be to learn about new work on your topic. I began to suspect—just suspect—that the information that I provided, useful though it was, was beginning to take a toll. And then, there was also a man. A dangerous looking man. Katherine said he was her friend." Ann raised her eyebrows inquiringly. "Now, could he have been responsible for the strange mail?"

"Strange mail?" I asked.

"She had other work, as well, you see. Not as creative as the Hitchcock but it paid a little something—reviewing proposals for an agent."

I had lingered long enough in her private world. "Yes," I said. It wasn't easy to keep my voice level. "I read one of those treatments."

"You?" she turned and faced me.

"How did you make the footers?"

"Footers?"

"The alternating footers in "The Hatchet Man.""

"The Hatchet Man," she repeated with a twisted smile.

"The story treatment you sent her. It was like a riddle, wasn't it? A familiar thing in unfamiliar guise. You made some interesting changes in the original, but you added something that was wrong."

The smile faded to a look of sharp calculation.

"What was that?"

"Behold, I come as a thief."

Now it was my turn.

She watched my face intently. "I don't understand," she said, but she understood perfectly.

"There were other collaborators on that story, though the original had a different title," I said. "Katy and I wrote it together."

"Katy?" Her eyes narrowed. "You mean Katherine? You knew her?"

I thought of the stolen frame with its family photos, like a fetish in her closet. Had she never suspected me—never despite my prodding about old books and inscriptions and about the subterranean creek, not even the echoes of "The Hatchet Man" in the story of Olivia, my very arrival there? That she was perceptive I had seen at once when I met her for the first time. But what I hadn't realized until now was that always on her mind was the past, and it was a burden that weighed on her and shadowed her vision.

She broke the silence. "Here's another riddle: what is black and red and white all over?"

Was she dangerous? I was past caring. "I give up," I said. "A Death Car."

Now, I saw.

"Katherine Marx was my cousin. Though, you know, it was *my* father—Roger, not Edward Marx—who drove a white car. It was a Cougar."

Her face went blank, and she stared at me.

Into my mind came the image of the brown cardboard box in the crowded confines of my father's garage. In the space once occupied by the white Cougar, I had first learned of the existence of the Kitteredge family. Now I learned, as had Graceann Kitteredge herself, that she had hounded to death the wrong person. The daughter of the man who had destroyed her family was not Katy Marx.

Chapter 26

Graceann Nilsson Kitteredge reached into a pocket of her Peruvian cardigan sweater and brought out a brown plastic pharmacy vial, removed the lid, and poured the contents into her hand—small green capsules that looked like little candies. Then she went into her bathroom. I heard water running into a glass. She came out and settled into her chair.

"My heart medication…digoxin gluconate," she said. "It comes from beautiful flowers—from foxglove."

I did not reply. What did I care? She had passed on her disease to me: she would have to live with the knowledge of her mistake, and I would have my hate of her—her, her cruelty, my uncle who made a mess trying to cover his brother's dirty tracks, my father, myself.

"It regulates the action of the heart muscle," she was saying. "Miraculous. But then, quite near the therapeutic level of dosage, toxicity occurs, and then death. The body tries to eliminate the toxic substance, because that is what it is, and nausea occurs, unless the dose is large enough to cause instantaneous heart failure."

She held up the pharmacy vial for me to see. It was upside down and empty.

"So you see, my medication has two possible functions— one is to keep me alive, and the other is not to."

I could have called for help, but I did not.

Ann's head drooped, and then her mouth gaped. She was staring at me.

"You were looking for something."

"Yes." I had been.

"The back collection? The books don't circulate. I'll take you back. I'll have to take you back. You can't go back alone. Look," and with a drunken gesture of the hand that took in the room, "All yellow—"

Nothing was yellow. It was dark in her room. It was dark outside. She was going.

I looked at the rug, not at her. I knew what had happened, and it happened quickly. If I had rushed for help the moment I saw the empty vial, I would not have reached the phone before she was dead. But I did not know that. Now her head rested on the back of the chair, and she was absolutely still, a frozen smile on her dead face, her lips drawn back in a leer.

I looked around the room. Both doors were locked, and I was, still, her prisoner. The key was in the pocket of her Peruvian sweater. I would have to get it. Would both locks use the same key?

The dead woman's hands were in her lap. I willed myself to lift the heavy, lifeless arm. I moved it to one side. It slid back down against the pocket. Try again. This time, I held the arm away from the body and reached into the pocket for the key.

I found the key and made it to the door leading outside. My hand shook. I got the key into the lock. It worked, and the door opened. The night, cold and black, was like a wall, and my face was suddenly hot. I stepped forward and missed the stairs. The hard ground came up to meet me, wet and smelling of juniper.

Chapter 27

Lorne found me.

Sarah had knocked on Ann's door and gotten no answer, so Lorne went down to check on the older woman. Ann was asleep, he said, but Sarah did not think so. Older people do not sleep soundly, Ann often had said. And Sarah had heard how loudly Lorne knocked on Ann's door, which was locked from the inside. Lorne, who generally made a point of ignoring his timid companion, this time went out the front door and down along the sloping side of the garden fence to look into Ann's room. He found me sitting in the mud leaning against the house with a bloody face. The garden door to Ann's room was open, and he found Ann in her chair.

Aliza got to San Francisco General at around 8:30 that night. A police inspector also came and asked me questions about Ann. But I was disoriented—my face hurt, and so did my head—I couldn't tell him much. I had an x-ray and got some medication.

I did not notice until we started for the car that Aliza's older teenage son had come with her. Her husband, a surgeon, had been on the job all day and needed to sleep. I had never seen Aliza looking so bad—tense and exhausted. I apologized to them, but I was grateful. We arrived back at my house at about 3:00 AM. Aliza slept on the couch.

She went home for a while in the morning, but came back and spent the day with me. While she was gone, a woman police inspector came and asked me questions. My head still hurt and throbbed when I moved it, which I soon learned to do only when absolutely necessary. Still, I was more or less ambulatory and able to take care of myself, so Aliza went home for the night.

Roger.

I had now to accept that the anger and resentment which I had always felt towards him, not without self-recrimination, had their foundation in truth. Revulsion worked its way through my system like poison.

The next day, I could drive. My still head hurt, especially when I moved it. Traffic was light on Lake Street that morning, and I was on the Bay Bridge in about twenty minutes. The City and the Bay glittered under dazzling clouds, but I found their beauty oppressive.

How would he take it? How much of the story did he know? Would he hear what I had to say and respond in the usual sardonic way? He would take it all in and make me feel wretched for having told him, for having presumed.

All of my life, this had been his response to me. No matter what I had to say, his reply would be off, always indirect, never fully responsive, usually subtly contemptuous. Always, irony or sarcasm hid him, and always came the point or way of looking at things that you could not have anticipated, the tangential element that he made central and fundamental, taking your argument and whatever feelings were attached to it and leaving you, instead, with something of his that you hadn't wanted and couldn't use. In other words, in the end, you got nothing.

An unfamiliar car was parked in front of the house—an old, brown VW van.

I climbed the flagstone steps, avoiding the thick tufts of weeds growing between the stones. Voices came from behind the house. A woman was laughing, and a man, not Roger, was talking in a raucous voice. I walked along the side of the house and out into the back garden where I could see the back of a large head of thick curly hair. Two men and the woman sat on lawn chairs bundled against the cold.

I recognized the flat acerbic voice of Martin Sawtelle, a former colleague of mine who had once been my father's student. He was an angry man of about forty-five who could not hold his liquor and had recently learned that he was one-eighth Blackfoot. The relatively new knowledge that he was descended from an oppressed people served—for him—to explain a lifetime of bitterness. He had once lived with a woman graduate student whose eardrum he ruptured during a beating.

"...banal and boring, but everybody clapped."

"Questions afterward," the woman intoned, aiming an admiring smile at Sawtelle.

"Oh, yes. Never mind the banality. The better to brown your nose with, my dears."

The wind died away for a moment, and they heard my footsteps rustling in the dead leaves on the grass. Sawtelle and his friend turned towards me, but my father seemed not to notice my arrival. All three were drinking beer from bottles.

"Hello, Dad."

He looked up at me from under the brim of his cap. His face appeared redder than usual, almost purple. His lips were pale.

"Ah. Bella," he said with a wan smile. "You know Martin."

I nodded and did not smile.

"And this is Barbara..." He waited for someone to fill in the insignificant detail.

"Mills," she said.

"Martin's friend. Barbara is doing work with Ellen Roth. Smollett, I think?"

"Sterne," the woman answered with a grin.

"Yes," Roger said. Then, not looking at me, he said, "Won't you sit down?" There wasn't a chair.

At last he looked at me. They all did.

"What happened to your face?" he asked casually. Part of it was blue.

"Oh, just a fall. Actually, I came to see you about something rather personal."

The *rather* was defensive, a typical concession to his inevitable disdain that made me sick of myself. Backing down again.

"Are we *de trop?*" Sawtelle asked pleasantly.

"Do you think we could go inside for moment, Dad?"

"Barbara," Sawtelle said, rising from his lounge chair, "we'll go in for a bit. We can find something to eat."

Without answering, the woman got up and followed him into the house.

I sat down sideways facing my father on Sawtelle's now vacant chair.

"I learned something about Katy's death."

His smile was pained. He did not invite me to continue.

"Her death was suicide only in a manner of speaking."

"In a manner of speaking?"

"In a way, she was murdered."

He no longer concealed his outright annoyance. "What nonsense. What on earth is this about, Bella?"

For a moment, I did not know. I never felt as alone as when I was with him.

"There was a woman—an older woman—who stalked Katy—I don't know a better term—and helped her die."

"What exactly do you mean?"

"This woman—I met her—knew that Katy was not well, and she exploited Katy's illness."

K. M. WOOD

"This sounds, if you'll forgive me..."

"Like one of my books? I thought you hadn't read any of them."

"Like Gothic fiction." He said, bored and looked towards the house.

"Not really. There is no erotic component."

For once, he looked mildly interested.

"Katy was only a surrogate, you see. The woman punished *her* because she could not punish a man who had committed a crime that wrecked her family and her life. It was years ago, 1966. And this man drove his car into her family's car, by accident, and drove away. He was probably a drunk who didn't even know what he had done, or if he did know, was too drunk to care.

"The accident, if you can call it that—reckless negligence is more like it—ruined the lives of the woman's husband and son. The son was badly injured and lived the rest of his life minus the higher brain functions. The father blamed himself for the boy's condition and committed suicide. Their name was Kitteredge."

His face betrayed no recognition.

"Doesn't ring a bell?"

"Should it?"

"Gregor Kitteredge was Uncle Edward's heir. You might recall my asking you about him and the $3 million dollar annuity."

"How do we know the driver was a man?" he asked disinterestedly.

The question was natural enough.

"The mother saw him. That is, she saw the car and saw that a man was driving. When certain information came into her hands about Uncle Edward, she concluded that he and the hit-and-run driver were the same person. Uncle Edward died before she could get to him. But she did succeed in locating Katy, and since someone would have to pay for what had been done to her family, she punished Katy. Did Graceann Kitteredge murder Katy? Did the man in the car murder Graceann Kitteredge's husband and son? You could say that the answer to both questions is yes."

Professor Roger Marx raised his eyebrows.

"Unfortunately," I said, "she murdered the wrong daughter."

For once, his expression was neutral—no irony, no sneer, no irritation at the pointless utterance of an intellectual inferior.

"She called it the Death Car. It was a white Cougar."

"You are implying something, Bella?"

"Not implying. You had a white Cougar."

"It was stolen and never recovered."

Again, the mind-souring sense of futility: the friendship renewed after Katy's death, pointless like the ministrations of paramedics arriving too late; my investigation—what else could I call it?—which in the end, revealed the guilt of my own father who, in apparent indifference to what I had said, seemed now on the point of falling asleep in his lawn chair.

"You are the one she wanted," I said. "It was you she hated, though she didn't know her mistake until just before she died. Edward's conscience spared you having to face consequences. But Katy was less fortunate."

Then, after a silence, the full force of a fury that I never had known before overwhelmed an entire lifetime of timidity where he was concerned. It gathered itself and broke over me. In a tone of the purest emotional neutrality, I said, "You must have forgotten the incident."

He rested his head against the back of his chair and looked up at the pale cirrus clouds floating overhead across the blue of the sky. "You have been busy," came the counter-accusation. "Have you discussed your discovery with anyone?"

My face, I remember, was impassive, at least I tried to make it so to cover my inwardly explosive reaction to his question, the positive exultation, the dizzying and altogether unaccustomed sense of power. Never had I experienced in his presence anything but the abject conviction of my own weakness and lack of worth. It was a conviction that neither achievement nor fullness of purse could diminish. Now, I was in a position to decide the course of his life.

I also saw at this moment, clearly and with certainty, that the festering infection, the pain that determined his every word and gesture was only his and that I was no longer to share it. I was separate from him. This suffering was all that we had ever shared.

"Do you mean the police?" I asked. Without waiting for his answer, I got up and walked away.

The heather growing at the side of the house needed trimming. Its branches scratched my legs and grabbed at my arms and hair as I made my way past them, going in more haste and with less care than I had used coming in. I glimpsed Martin Sawtelle and his friend eating sandwiches in the kitchen, but I did not wave goodbye to them.

Chapter 28

The morning outside was bright and clear. Inspector Elena Kalatzis looked out across the water at the waves breaking against the Marin Headlands and the great orange bridge suspended in the air off to the east. Her dark, intelligent, rather sorrowful face did not betray whether or not she could tell I'd not been altogether candid with her. She had arrived for the first time the day after Ann's death—as it happened, while Aliza was gone—and by then, I felt well enough to tell her about finding Katy. I told her about "The Hatchet Man" and where it had taken me. But this had not been a complete account.

I had been involved in two suicides. I was a person of interest in one of them, Katy's. Now I had been cleared of any involvement in Ann's death.

The police found Katy's family pictures in the basement closet. The information I'd given at the hospital had been confirmed. Graceann Nilsson Kitteredge's digoxin gluconate was refillable monthly. The bathroom glass and medication vial had only her fingerprints on them. The mother of Katy Marx' landlady in Venice had positively identified Graceann from a DMV photo as someone who had frequently visited the deceased tenant, Katherine Marx. Inspector Kalatzis returned the pouch and "The Hatchet Man." Edward Marx' attorney, the administrator of his estate, corroborated my statement about the annuity benefiting Gregor Kitteredge, deceased.

In my earlier life I could never have imagined myself lying to the police, and my omission of information about Roger Marx and his white Cougar was the same as a lie.

Now, Inspector Kalatzis rose and shook my hand, as I hoped, for the last time. Pristine ocean air blew into my living room when she opened the door. She lingered for a moment on the porch, taking in the view, and I had a moment's apprehension that she would come back inside and the whole tiring, grim business of talking and answering questions would be renewed. But she left, and I heard her footsteps descending the stairs, and the worry of the last few weeks lifted from me like a garment of lead.

My head throbbed. I went to the kitchen and took my pill a little early.

Inspector Kalatzis had brought up my mail—a few bills and a large envelope with a 48th Avenue return address. Inside was a manuscript, its 30 or so pages held together by a large binder clip. Enclosed was a note: "I found this in Ann's room and thought you must have left it there. Take care, Mimi."

It was not finished after all.

What if, I asked myself, I had not gone to visit Katy? Had not exhumed, so to speak, at least some of the truth surrounding her death? What if I just threw this envelope and its contents away, or burned them, or shredded them? But I had learned something about myself. I've got to know.

Zero Balance: An Old Woman's Story

Even now, I remember, the last normal day of my life, an overcast June morning in Los Angeles, 1957.

I liked to swim before breakfast and that morning, went in early, at around 7:00. It was quiet, except for the doves calling and the plashing of the water against the sides of the pool as I swam. The two huge bougainvilleas—purple and orange—were especially beautiful this morning, blazing against a white sky. From down below, at the bottom of the garden, came the sound of dishes being set out for breakfast on the patio. The letter from Cal admitting me to graduate school was in my shirt pocket, a talisman.

I wanted very much to go, but going would have to wait until next year. I had decided to stay at home for now, just to be with my parents during my uncle's illness, and, we knew, his illness was nearing its end. Mother and Dad never would have asked me to stay, but I knew that I could help them. They argued with me when I told them my decision to postpone leaving, but they were grateful.

At first, my uncle had his own room, and although he was visibly weakening, he could still get up and down stairs and with help could even use the pool. After a month or so, though, he became too weak for physical activity, so my parents installed him in the den, and he used the guest bathroom, which had its own shower. The change that came over our household was entirely predictable but, even now, difficult to describe, because it was as though the lights gradually went out and the atmosphere grew heavy. My parents continued their usual good-natured banter with each other, my uncle, and everybody else. Mother enrolled in cooking school and began making special meals to revive my uncle's appetite. This strategy worked for a while, with the unintended consequence that Dad gained weight. I would have, too, but—mainly to preserve a positive state of mind—I doubled up on tennis and swimming. Mother's weight did not increase. They had fewer parties, and finally none at all. Uncle Dennis had a full time attendant, but we always checked him once or twice during the night.

When he was no longer able to leave the den, and even before that, he liked me to read to him, especially Dickens. We took turns reading to each other, at least at first, and dramatically rendering the voices of the various characters. When he grew very ill, I did the reading, and he listened or dozed off.

My father was with him when he died. It was evening, and they had both dozed off—Dad from fatigue and Uncle Dennis from morphine—and when Dad woke, his brother was gone.

Hundreds attended my uncle's funeral. Many were there for my parents. But there were also Uncle Dennis' friends, colleagues, and grateful patients. My friends were also there.

After the funeral, there was a large catered gathering at home, and after that, the house seemed empty. Fall came bringing with it hot days and stagnant air.

Mother and Dad went to Italy, but I stayed home. It seemed like a good idea for them to have some time together to recover, and I could keep an eye on the redecorating that Mother had arranged to cheer us all up. I had put off starting Cal as an Art History graduate student until the next fall. Even though Uncle Dennis had died during the summer, it was now too late to go.

You shouldn't assume that putting off graduate school was easy or painless. It wasn't. It was a difficult decision, but my parents needed me, and I never regretted staying. One of the vexing things about it, though, was that my boyfriend had applied to the UC Journalism School to be with me. He left, and when he had been in Berkeley for a few weeks, found someone new, and that was the end of that. This was an unpleasant development, but I managed to recover.

While the redecorating was underway, my uncle Marcus, the production designer, offered me an apprenticeship in his new project, a movie about the merchant service in World War II on the Murmansk route. Marcus had been trained as a painter. His sets were spectacularly beautiful and often looked like paintings. He had worked with several great directors and cameramen and his concepts—especially the use of light—had been faithfully rendered onscreen. The movie about the Murmansk route was not really in this category, but it was a good way for me to learn production design, and

I was glad to have the opportunity. The work was demanding, and the hours were brutal, but I loved the work, and I liked working for my uncle. He was a driven man, but an excellent teacher. It seemed to me that I had landed in the right place.

I worked with Marcus again, the next time on a movie about the last days of the Hapsburg Empire. This project called on all of my uncle's immense experience as an artist and art historian, but it turned out to be a problem for me. He never stopped working, so neither did I. Marcus thrived on the mad, unrelenting work schedule. I tried hard to follow his example and almost made it through the entire production. But just at the end, I became ill with pneumonia, which led to a weakening of the heart. Mother and Dad were incensed with Marcus, who had given me a wonderful professional opportunity and couldn't help being totally immersed in a project that he loved. He became, for a time, anathema to them, an adder in their midst. Once I had recovered and began to put on weight and look less and less cadaverous as time went on, I was ready to work for him again. But my brief, happy career in production design was over. The medical opinion was that I couldn't tolerate intense stress and over-work and would have to make my way in life in a quieter profession. I took this bitter and thwarting news poorly.

One night, I lay awake in my room. There was a full moon, and its light streamed in through one of my windows turning the blue chintz flowers on the window seat to silver. Mother and Dad came in. They sat on the window seat and didn't speak. I pretended to be asleep. They just sat there. Were they waiting for a bus? I stubbornly kept my eyes closed, breathed quietly and evenly, and lay very still. At last, Mother said, as though we were sitting over coffee, "Your father has had an Idea." Then they said nothing. I tried to ignore them, but it was no use. She was like a predatory animal. She could always tell when I was faking sleep. It was the same when I was trying to get out of school or any other burdensome thing, and she always could tell. I opened my eyes.

Their Idea: library school! I was speechless. How had they come up with this? They explained. They had looked through the Berkeley catalogue and found a subject that was as different as possible from Industry work and within my range of abilities and consistent with my experience in that I had always liked books. It was as though they had suggested a career in major league baseball or the Cloth. But, they pointed out, I could be in Berkeley. Art History was fine, too, but if I wasn't planning on a career in movie production, was that field a good choice? I didn't tell them that I had by no means permanently abandoned production design. They would not have accepted anything short of changing professions to help my damaged heart. But to give up production design would have caused a different kind of damage. There would be time much later on to discuss this point with them. But not now. I promised to look into library school and went to sleep with them still sitting on the window seat in the moonlight.

In Berkeley, I found a nice room in a large house in the Hills. It had its own tennis court, and my landlord, a widower, said that if I gave him tennis lessons, I could use the court to give lessons to students of my own. This was just what I needed, because I wanted some financial independence. After all, I was 23, and my parents, although comfortably off, should not be supporting me for the rest of my life. Then, too, financial independence of any degree would make it easier for me to deal with them when the time came for me to return to work in production design. It turned out to be easy enough to attract a few students just by posting note cards around the campus. I acquired four students, and the income from their lessons enabled me to lower my allowance by almost 50%. My parents, predictably, said that they would put the other 50% in an account for me. I objected, but in the end, they won out, although Mother was to use that money later on.

The UC School of Library Science, as it was called in those days, was pleasant and peaceful, although at first, and even as time went on, my life felt a little like an out-of-body experience, with one self observing, without being part of, the other. I had come from a place where high value was placed on imagination, idiosyncrasy, and unpredictability. Now, here I was in a place where system regularity and predictability were everything. How on earth had that happened? I loved where I had come from and meant to go back. I missed art. But this was my own place. I had been brought up to be independent in just about every way and to have confidence in myself and my decisions. So here I was, and—to make my parents happy for the time being—here I would stay until I became a librarian. I felt sure that my health would improve and that my uncle would find something for me by and by. I was fully capable of going my own way, whatever my parents should think, but rebellion for its own sake had no value for me.

It was a one-year program, and the skills and degree would be good to have, even though I had never really believed that there was anything wrong with my heart. A year in Berkeley learning something new and teaching tennis on the side wouldn't be such a bad thing. Berkeley was lovely and idyllic then, in 1958, and the Library Science program was so very different from my life in LA, that my time there would be a restful interlude.

Order was all. It was our god. There was a supremely logical and perfect System which accounted for all available information. My fellow students were quiet people, unobtrusive, polite, and intense where devotion to the System was concerned. These were not people like my parents' friends who jumped in their cars at 2:00 AM to shop for watermelon after a nighttime swim in the nude. But I liked my fellow students, and two became my tennis pupils.

The following January, Dad had a heart attack and almost died. In the pre-Medicare era, serious illness could create a serious financial burden. Although my parents assured me that they had the financial resources to continue their current way of living, I felt that I needed to help, and looking around for new means of support, I discovered that, although I had no teaching credential (and no desire for one) I was qualified to work as a substitute teacher in Berkeley's public school system. I could accept assignment calls or not, depending on my own needs, and this arrangement seemed an ideal way to supplement the tennis-teaching revenues.

So I began at a middle school with children who at that time were beginning to be called disadvantaged, a euphemism that hardly applied to the mind-numbing chaos of my classrooms filled with children who had nothing other than absent, struggling, and in some cases criminal parents and who were semi-literate at best. They were undisciplined and some were downright dangerous, and naturally, like all schoolchildren, they missed no opportunity to exploit and persecute the substitute teacher. My job was mainly custodial.

The substitute teaching was a grubby business, and yet, I felt strangely drawn to the work. No, that's not quite it. It awakened in me a sense of my privileges, of the enriched and amusing life that I had always known which had never involved anything dismal or sordid. These children belonged to a dismal and sordid world that had given them only one opportunity to improve their condition: the public school classroom, and for that, they were completely unprepared. They had neither the mental background nor the behavior to benefit from school. I never had intended to stay, yet something—social guilt, I guess—made me continue on through the summer. My plan for after graduation was to work as a librarian for a year or so, thus avoiding adding to my parents' worries and relieving them of financial responsibility for me, and then, no matter what, back to production design.

But that summer, I met Justin Davis, a math teacher with a grim social conscience. He had grown up in poverty in Philadelphia with a mentally ill and alcoholic mother. Looking back, there was no evidence at all that he and I were compatible. But I was younger emotionally than I realized and was attracted to what I must have perceived as his emotional need without understanding that certain needs cannot be met in a healthy way by another's love. I lived with him for two years, during which time I had little contact with my parents and my old life and was emotionally blackmailed by Justin into continuing the grueling substitute teaching routine, because he believed librarianship to be an elitist profession.

That winter, Dad had a massive and fatal heart attack. Justin again used emotional blackmail, his specialty, to prevent my going to LA for more than an overnight. Looking back on my time with him, I can't recognize myself in the person I had become.

When President Kennedy created the Peace Corps, Justin volunteered and went to Africa. I never saw him again. When he told me his plans, I was devastated. I had entirely subordinated myself to him and, always trying to make it good, was incapable of admitting to myself how bleak and sterile this all was. But to my amazement, when he had packed his few possessions and left, almost immediately came a terrific and entirely unanticipated sense of relief and exhilaration that I hadn't experienced since meeting him.

My first act was to move out of the West Berkeley basement apartment that he and I had shared and into a studio pretty far up Euclid in the Berkeley Hills. I bought a bicycle and applied for work in the University Library system, the Berkeley Public Library, and at a couple of law firms. To my amazement, almost immediately I went to work in what then was then called the Oriental Languages Library set in a small and elegant room in Durant Hall. What a liberating and enjoyable job and life! I went back to tennis-teaching and playing where I had started out, at the private court in the Hills. But before starting the new job, I went to visit Mother.

She and I looked at each other thinking the same thing: we both looked terrible. The main difference between our respective ordeals, though, was that Mother had not betrayed anyone, as I had done. She was thin and pale, had not, as I learned from the housekeeper, been eating well, and spent most of her time watching television. She slept little, going to bed late and getting up early. I withdrew the funds from the account that Mother and Dad started for me and deposited them in hers. She was too worn out to notice the new deposit. Less than a year after my father died, she joined him.

Our house had been left to me, and I put it on the market. I remember the last day before the new owners took possession, sitting all day in June overcast by the pool, listening to the water lapping at the sides, knowing I could never come back. I hated the man who hid his mean nature behind the pretense of social conscience.

I was alone in the house now. Marcella, the housekeeper of many years, had been gone for a month. Most of my parents' things had been sold at auction, and, like the proceeds from the house sale, went to pay their debts, mainly medical expenses. I went back to Berkeley and started my new job with a heavy and bitter sense of loss.

But the Oriental Languages Library was healing place—beautiful and silent with glowing, polished wood furnishings from an earlier time and usually sparsely populated. Many of the users were foreign students from Germany who had been attracted to Berkeley by the University's renowned Oriental Languages program. By and large, they were an unprepossessing lot and not especially robust.

But there was one exception. Julian Kitteredge was tall, dark and well built. He looked a bit like Gregory Peck, was a few years older than the others, had lived in Japan, and was fluent in Japanese. He was fascinated by Tibetan and was trying to learn it along with Mandarin. He also wanted eventually to learn Mongolian. Studying these languages was a labor of love for him, but his parents wanted him to major in Business Administration and return to Albany, New York to run the family drug store chain. He had been thinking over what to do, and so had also been taking classes in Business Administration. We had coffee a few times, and he signed up for tennis lessons, which he did not need, in less than a minute demonstrating that he was a faster and more accurate player than his teacher. We began seeing each other seriously and were married after a year.

We went east to Albany to be married, and at first I got along well with Julian's parents, who saw me as a beneficial influence in the direction of Business Administration and family responsibility. I was, of course, a strong believer in the latter, but as to Julian's career plans, well, I was—as my parents had taught me to be—an advocate for following the heart. Eventually, this fact became known to my in-laws, and their feelings for me cooled. Julian applied to the Oriental Languages graduate program, and I transferred to the Main Library Reference Desk.

The next year, our son was born. This was not a planned birth, as Julian was working towards the doctorate and had only part-time work as a research assistant. I went on a short maternity leave and then returned to work part-time, so that Julian and I could share caring for Gregor. Eventually we co-ordinated things so well that I was also able to pick up a little additional income by teaching tennis during the longer summer evenings.

Julian's professor, Gustav Ehrhardt, and his wife occasionally invited us to dinner, and on one occasion—it was Halloween—we went to the Ehrhardts' and took Gregor along. The dinner was fun. Mrs. Ehrhardt made a wonderful sauerbraten and for dessert, a delicious apfeltorte. The other guest was a star graduate student from Essen who maintained silence throughout the evening and appeared to be catatonic, except that he ate his way through several helpings of each course.

We left at around 11:00. Northampton Avenue was always quiet. But now, it was completely deserted. Trick-or-treating had been over for hours. There was no moon that perfectly clear, windy, cloudless night and no streetlights anywhere near us. The houses were all set far back from the street—downhill on one side, uphill on the other, and there were trees and shrubs everywhere. Professor Ehrhardt told us about his neighbor, a professor of Economics, whose house had been burglarized three times. The police had told him to cut back his shrubbery so that the house could be seen from the street, but No, he had said—and Professor Ehrhardt warmly agreed—they liked the privacy, not to mention the beautiful trees.

There were a million stars, and in the wind, they seemed to be racing across the sky. We stood for a long moment watching them. The trees thrashed about in the wind and made a rushing sound like a river. One had the sense of owning that night and that place.

Julian was carrying Gregor, who somehow had remained asleep after being picked up from his borrowed bed, talked over as we said goodnight, and carried out into the cold. A hawthorn hedge grew along the curb and blocked the car's rear door. "If I pull away from the curb, I'll have to hand him off to you, and he might wake up," Julian said. "That's OK," I answered, "he'll go right to sleep as soon as we start driving." But Julian had already started into the street. I never, ever, loaded Gregor on the street side of the car. It was too late, though, to object, because Julian, still carrying Gregor, had unlocked the car and gotten the rear door open.

Indistinguishable from the wind, the rush of the speeding car was inaudible until it came into view careening around the curve in the road. One of its headlights was out.

It was heading straight for our car. I stared at it. Inconceivable that it would not correct its course at the last instant and pass us safely. And it did pass us, without stopping after the deafening crash of the impact when it smashed into our car, Julian, and Gregor. I was sitting on the curb in shock when the Ehrhardts and their neighbors came running out of their houses and found us. I did not know where Julian and Gregor were.

Afterwards, over and over, I asked myself, what if I had called out to Julian that night: DON'T TAKE HIM INTO THE STREET? What if I had disturbed that windy night and called out in a voice of command or shrill protest that I never had used? Julian, would have stopped, looked at me in surprise or shock—even annoyance—but I would have stopped him. He would then have pulled the car away from the curb making space for me to load Gregor on the curb side. Then, if the other car had hit us, Gregor would have been spared, and the armor of our car would have given Julian some protection.

The next years were dark and difficult. The collision left Julian with a spinal injury and chronic pain. Gregor had brain damage, and we were told that we would not be able to care for him at home. Julian continued on with graduate school, but now the work was terribly challenging because of his back pain. And guilt, because *he* had taken Gregor into the street. Our son no longer seemed to know either of us. But we knew him. We loved him, but he did not know us. He could walk and feed himself fairly well, but toilet habits were a problem, and seizures were terrifying. There was a fine residential treatment facility near Davis, and he was accepted there. Money, as we were told, from a special philanthropic fund made this arrangement possible. There were other facilities, but this one was the best, and we never could have afforded it on our own. We visited Gregor every weekend.

Julian never complained about pain, and he kept his guilt feelings to himself. But these two problems were barriers to his work, and he began to fail. On the evening of the second anniversary of the crash—Halloween, again—as I turned onto Walnut Street from Hearst, I could see that the front window of our flat was dark. In those days, anything unusual made me sick with dread. I felt, as I had so many times since the accident, the familiar clenched stomach, but as I had gotten into the habit of doing, I told myself to calm down. Julian was napping or in the kitchen—or possibly even not at home—I was always pushing him to take walks to help control the back pain.

The hallway was full of the smell of onion cooking in the flat upstairs. I unlocked our door and went in. In earlier times, this had been a family home, and our dining room had been the family dining room. It had a high ceiling and exposed beams. No lights at all were on in the flat. But of course, darkness in cities is never absolute. There was a glow from the streetlights outside, and inside was Julian, his long, graceful form suspended from a ceiling beam by a length of clothesline that made a noose around his throat.

I was careful to tell Gregor in the proper way. He was six years old. Daddy had an accident and would not be coming back, I told him, watching his beautiful face for the response that did not come. Gregor's staff counselor had cautioned me that he would not respond, but I privately had hoped for some glimmer of human emotion. In fact, this was the pattern that had established itself in all of Julian's and my visits to Gregor: hope that was completely unfounded and was, always, destroyed by the actual encounter. Julian's parents came for his funeral and went home again. They did not visit their grandchild and barely spoke to me.

I stayed on in the flat until our lease was up, took a temporary post at Davis to be near Gregor, and then moved back to Berkeley when a position became available, this time in the Bancroft Library. Anything removed from old associations would suit me. It was then that I began to live without a permanent home and embarked on what turned out to be a decades-long career of house-sitting for faculty and University administrators on sabbatical. I became a kind of nomad, or fugitive.

A few weeks before his 21st birthday, Gregor had an unusually violent seizure and died. Was it a relief no longer to worry about his wellbeing? Or no longer to live with the pain of loving my son who did not know me and with the constant reminders of everything that he—really, that he, Julian, and I—had missed? It was not, not then, because the bond had been strong. His death was a grievous loss, and the calamity that had been his life had only strengthened the attachment.

I now was without human ties.

I joined a grief support group and began to experience, as I thought at the time, some relief. I went back to tennis, trying mentally to reconnect with the old LA days. My parents and uncles were gone, but there was still tennis, and I joined a group of older and middle aged women who played twice each week at Strawberry Canyon. I got into the habit of swimming afterwards, even on cold days. My house sitting jobs were in the Berkeley Hills or in the Claremont District, and I began walking to work each day, rain or shine, and to feel better, more like my old self before coming to Berkeley such a long time ago. For the first time in more than thirty years, I was taking care of myself, I thought.

I developed a following of house-sitting clients among faculty and administrators. I was paid stipends, but the real financial benefit was not paying rent. The homes were always large and attractive. Professor Glick (Mathematics) had hardly any furniture, but a spectacular view to the West. So did Mrs. Rhust, 76 years of age, who worked in the Chancellor's office and lived on the uphill side of Cragmont Avenue in a house with a terrace that looked straight out at San Francisco and the Golden Gate Bridge. She traveled every year and, as an inducement for me to be available when she needed me, made a garden bedroom and bath mine to use as her guest between house-sitting jobs.

I had gotten through the bad time with Justin and had survived a catastrophic family situation that ended in the deaths of the two people I loved. I had been the best mother that I could be to a severely disabled son to whom I had been a stranger. I now had plenty of friendly relationships—the

tennis group, co-workers at the Bancroft, fellow swimmers—
and I saw people occasionally when one or the other group
got together, but there were no real friendships and no relationships with men. I was safe.

But I had a problem, which I should have suspected
from this lack of any close relationships. Moving like a frigid, deep current at the bottom of the sea—despite tennis,
swimming, walking and cycling everywhere, companion-
able activities, and general sense of moving forward— the
cycle of grieving, relief, and remorse ground on. All the
while, as I lived quietly and usefully, a dagger twisted in my
heart.

I decided to leave Berkeley for new surroundings not
charged with the old, sad memories. As I was thinking over
what I might do, a co-worker brought up her own plan for a
change of direction. She and her partner had their eye on a
large house in San Francisco. They would rent out rooms and
were looking for a co-investor. Was I interested? I decided
to join them, and we worked out an arrangement whereby I
would co-own the property, but they would have full responsibility for managing it and for the many improvements that
it needed. They also planned to provide meals. It would be
like an old-fashioned boarding-house. The house overlooked
Ocean Beach from the top of a bluff called Sutro Heights. I
would live in the lower portion of the house, which had been
converted to a bed-sitting room with its own entrance and
bath, and would live there off-and-on until leaving house-
sitting altogether, which I thought would happen when I retired from the University.

One night at Mrs. Rhust's house, my shoulder and jaw began to hurt and then chest pains started, and I was a 911 call. It was my old post-pneumonia problem, and after two months on disability, I decided to retire and move to the house in San Francisco.

As a nomad I had accumulated few possessions: clothes, tennis racquets—would I ever be able to play again?—books, a laptop. There were also some things of Julian's, including his collection of children's books from childhood. I never had been able to part with his old wallet, and I took it along with me. But I threw out a lot during the packing, and although some unneeded odds and ends traveled with me to the new house, a rented pick-up hauled all of my possessions in one trip. It was January, and I gave Mrs. Rhust a bare-root Joseph's Coat as a thank you gift.

The 1926 Sutro Heights house had four bedrooms and a large bathroom, all on the top floor. It sat on a downward-sloping lot facing the ocean and, at some point before World War II, a greenhouse on the basement level had been converted to a bedroom and small bathroom. There was also a closet which extended back into the unfinished basement. The house had been emptied of furnishings when we took possession, but a few old pieces remained, and among them was a chest of drawers, which had been placed in the closet for me.

Our house in Bel Air had been large, casually furnished (at considerable expense), and full of light. And here I was, after nearly 40 years, albeit in smaller quarters, again in a light-filled space with the vast Pacific Ocean as my backyard neighbor. After many, many years, I still remembered one of my early questions to my uncle about set design: "Which painter would have painted this room?" (His only answer would be a smile.) Now, I thought, my room and its view could have been in a Matisse oil with the windows at the center open to the sea beyond.

Librarians are devoted to order, but I never had been, at heart, of their race. To myself, I felt again that I was an artist—a set designer, but without a set. Always in other peoples' homes, I had no opportunity to create a set for my own life. Now, in the studio apartment overlooking the Pacific, I would have that opportunity. The light there was very good—direct from the west in the afternoon, indirect from the north throughout the day. The blues, grays, and violets of the seascape and the greens of the open spaces surrounding the house—not to mention the sunset roses, coppers, and golds—would be all the color I'd need. The interior would be white, all white.

My new bed had arrived before me and very kindly had been set up by my business partners. I unpacked my clothes. The rest—books and music, mostly—would wait until I had found the right furnishings. One box that I had stored at Mrs. Rhust's contained old files—mostly financial documents, and some more recent papers that I'd been in too much of a hurry to sort through before packing. I made myself a cup of tea upstairs in the kitchen and came back downstairs to sit on the bed and watch the ocean. Heavy clouds hung above the gray-green expanse. I could hear the screaming of gulls. What a long time since I had been to the beach—any beach—and how different this one from benign Santa Monica where I had spent my summers—different, but beautiful and with its own restorative power.

I pulled off the packing tape, opened the box, and began sorting the contents. There were the bank statements, tax records, and UC employment documents to be organized by date and type. There was my old, expired, and never used passport and the carved sandalwood box from India containing photos of Julian, Gregor, and me, none from the time after the crash, and unopened since that time. Also in the box: Julian's old wallet.

In all these years, I had never opened the wallet, but now, I looked inside. Its contents were frayed and bent to the shape of the wallet, everything just as it had been when he died such a long time ago. His driver's license, his university registration card, a five dollar bill, a supermarket check-cashing privileges card, and something else: some newspaper clippings folded into a small, very bulky square. I counted them. There were seven, seven clippings meticulously folded and jammed into Julian's wallet. One was a fragment of a map, and there were bits of news items about an earthquake in Tashkent, of all things, and, to my sorrow, two pieces about our crash. That moment brought the frightful image of Julian, inwardly disintegrating, alone, fitfully cutting out scraps of newspaper, horrible mementos of the crash and its consequences. The earthquake? I knew Julian, and now what came back to me after all of the years since he died was his habit of placing problems "in perspective," as he would say. We had experienced calamity. But others—the thousands made homeless in Tashkent, according to one of the articles—how I remembered—how much worse for them!

But how much worse than I ever had suspected was the whole aftermath of the crash for him. The suffering that he had hidden from me struck me as never before. One of the clippings had a black blot on it. Oh yes. I knew the cause: shoe polish. Julian was always so careful about his shoes. Not fussy, but careful, and he polished them regularly. The clippings hauled me mercilessly back to that time. I put them back in the wallet and buried the wallet under clothes in a drawer, then drank some tea, and got back to work.

Some old junk mail had found its way into this box, some of it very old indeed, overlooked as I had put other papers in the box, my only document storage for many years. Among these was something—a letter—from a bank. But this letter was not for me. Someone else's name appeared above my address in the envelope window and in the letter itself—a data sorting error of some kind. When I opened it, I saw that it was not junk mail. The letter, dated 1983, was addressed to a Mr. Edward Marx, Marx, Unwin & Salinger, LLP and advised Mr. Marx that the annuity payments to Primary Beneficiary Gregor Kitteredge had, owing to Mr. Kitteredge's demise, been discontinued.

I sat on my bed, now re-reading the letter, now staring at nothing.

Dusk came on. The sun had hidden all day behind dark clouds. Now it appeared fiery copper at the horizon. It faded to a lurid glow, and disappeared into the sea. Night fell. Nothing existed but this letter. I was lost in it, stunned by the sudden intrusion of someone I did not know, someone of whom I had never heard, into the most private and dreadful part of my life.

Edward Marx. What had he to do with us—with the Us of whom I was the sole survivor?

LLP: a law firm. Attorneys sometimes administer annuities. Julian's parents had not attended Gregor's funeral, and I complied with what I thought was their wish to avoid us. I did not communicate with them.

But had I misjudged my in-laws? Julian died in 1968, and his funeral was the last time I'd seen or heard from them. If they had been supporting their grandson in the best available facility, even if they couldn't face seeing him or me, wouldn't they at least have told me? I had been a reminder of Gregor's condition and Julian's suicide. This I knew. But could there, after all, have been something else preventing them from at least acknowledging Gregor's death in 1983? I went back to my laptop and searched for the *Van Buren Voice* and then for their names.

There was indeed another reason. Julian's mother had died in 1974 and his father in 1979.

Now that I thought about this whole business, wouldn't I have been notified, at some point, when payments from an annuity ended? And how had they started?

There had been so much pain and confusion at that terrible time. Julian and I could hardly talk to each other. Each of us was a raw nerve. The day we learned that Gregor would always need care and would never live independently—this was a day that I had tried to forget. A hospital social worker talked with us about care facilities and found a place for Gregor at a facility called The Lodge. It was in the Sierra Foothills, and Julian and I went to see it.

The place looked like a resort. It was clean and attractive. There were gardens and lawns. There was even a tennis court. The children lived in bungalows each with a staff counselor. Advanced medical care was on site. It looked excellent, for what it was. But it was not home, and the thought of leaving our child there was almost unendurable. And the cost was beyond our capability. There was, so we were told, a foundation that could help with support for Gregor. We weren't in any condition to make further inquiries. We accepted the terms, and Gregor went to live there and never came out. I remember thinking that Julian had asked his parents for help, but I did not ask him about this. The subject of his relationship with them was too sensitive to bring up at the time, and I didn't have the strength of mind to do it.

I never admitted to myself that I disliked and resented my in-laws. They disapproved of a Hollywood background, but accepted me until Julian decided not to join the family business. They had loved Gregor, but turned away after the crash. And would the crash have happened if not for graduate school? If not for whatever encouragement I had given to Julian's Sino-Tibetan ambitions that brought him to the Ehrhardts' house on the last good night of our lives?

My thoughts drifted. Had I been unfair or even cruel? What if I had reached out to Julian's family? What if I had tried to have a relationship with them? It could have been a good thing for all of us. I had lived without attachments for so many years. I could scarcely imagine what a relationship with Julian's parents would have been like—visits to Upstate New York, presents or cards at holidays, phone calls from time to time? In view of this letter and the *Van Buren Voice* obituaries, I had made a serious miscalculation.

The bus stop near my new home was the end of the line for the #38 Geary bus, which, I learned, crosses San Francisco from west to east and back again. After a night of disturbed sleep, at 8:00 or so the next morning, I climbed aboard. The offices of Marx, Unwin & Salinger were in the Merchants' Exchange Building, and they were open for business when I arrived. A woman of about my age with steel gray hair in a bun sat behind a large desk and seemed troubled when I asked to see Mr. Marx. She told me that Mr. Marx was deceased. I must have looked stricken, because she stood up and apologized for the sad news. Would I like a glass of water? Would I sit down?

This was a blow. Since finding the letter, all I'd been able to think of was talking with Edward Marx and learning the truth about Julian's parents, although even if I had been wrong about them and had repaid their generosity with cold-ness and distance, the chance to mend things had passed out of reach long ago. I sat on the couch in the reception area, and the receptionist brought me water in a paper cup. Then she sat down with me. "Were you a client of Mr. Marx?"

"No, but I believe that my late in-laws were his clients. I wanted to see him about an annuity that I believe Mr. Marx administered for them."

She looked at me curiously. "Annuity?"

"I know that that information would be confidential. But I thought that he might be able to help in some way."

The woman looked at me with concern. "You know," she said, "Mr. Marx had corporate clients. I don't think that he was ever involved with annuity administration. Perhaps I could check for you, just in a general way." She disappeared, and I waited.

When she came back, she said that Mr. Unwin had told her that Edward Marx did not manage annuities. None at all. Mr. Unwin would be glad to make a referral, if I needed help in that field.

Outside, a cable car came by and I got on and rode to Van Ness. Then I walked to Geary and got on the bus for home.

Back in my room, I read the letter from the bank again: "…your account #XXXX-XXXX." Your account. The annuity payments to beneficiary Gregor Kitteredge. How many possible meanings were there? Just the one. Edward Marx was involved in the crash. This had to be it. He might even have been the driver and had taken it upon himself to make restitution in his own and very private way. Now, no one could ask him.

That afternoon, my business partners took me shopping for furniture. We spent the rest of that day and part of the next shopping for a desk, chairs, lamps, and rug. I tried to forget about my in-laws and Edward Marx. It was too late to make amends to Julian's parents, if amends were needed. But the mystery of Edward Marx—whoever he was—was impossible to ignore. Thinking about it became a kind of chronic disease, a painful condition that only knowing about him would remedy.

The furniture shopping was tiring, and I had to make some compromises, but at least my room would be comfortable. We were all glad to have finished, and we were home early in the afternoon on the second day. I found the phone directory and looked for Edward Marx in the residential section, but he was not listed.

By 2:30, under an ominous sky with rain due, I was back on the bus. I got off at Van Ness and started towards the Civic Center. I found the phone directories on the 5th floor of the Main Library. Edward Marx had last listed his home and phone number in 1985. His house was on 30th Avenue, just a few blocks from Geary. On my way home, I got off at the 33rd Avenue stop and walked back eastward to 30th.

I had never gotten to know San Francisco well, and the Richmond District was especially unfamiliar to me. But Edward Marx' neighborhood was unlike any other that I'd seen in the City. The houses were large and substantial and set well back from the street on spacious lots. There was none of the urban crowding together that one saw almost everywhere else in San Francisco, even in expensive neighborhoods. These were well-maintained stucco and shingled homes.

Lights were going on inside the houses. Some still had holiday lights sparkling in their gardens and wreaths still on their doors. They looked inviting. But Edward Marx's house was dark. Its windows were bare, and it looked empty. I walked back to Geary and waited for the bus.

On the way, I passed a tennis court. Yes, I know. I had a weak heart. But I still loved tennis, and I thought that a little practice—just against a backboard—would be safe enough—nothing too exerting. Plus, I'd walk at least some of the way to the courts, a mile or so each way, which would help me towards whatever conditioning I was capable of. There was risk involved—true—but for me, even at my age, an inactive life was not worth much. The next morning, I found my racquet and an unopened can of balls. Just ten or so blocks from home were the Cabrillo courts—39th and Fulton. But I took the bus to 33rd Avenue and walked the rest of the way to the courts on 30th near Clement.

I took it easy and enjoyed myself. So many things had changed in a short time. I was no longer working. I no longer lived in Berkeley, where I had lived for decades. I now had a fixed home. I lived with other people. (I was not sure how this would work out, but I would give myself some time to get used to it.) But tennis was an old friend still waiting for me. On the way home, I took a detour past the Marx house. It looked sad in the light of a gray morning.

It rained all the next day. The courts would be wet, so there was no chance of tennis practice. After that, though, I practiced most days, and always at 30th Avenue. My route unvaryingly took me past the Marx house. No, it was not on my way, but the additional walking was healthful. Once, a gardener was trimming the hedges. Once, I saw a woman inside cleaning, and once, as I was heading home after a late afternoon practice, I saw refuse bins and bags outside the house and on the front lawn, a For Sale sign that gave me a stab of anger.

First Edward Marx and then his house had given me a connection with the past: now both were lost. I realized in that moment that I had never recovered from the terrible events of my life because they had been a mystery. I had never learned the identity of the person responsible for them, and no one had ever been brought to justice.

It started to rain as I stood at the end of the block and looked back at the bins in front of the Marx house. Then I walked back. Perfectly nice, respectable people went through bins. I recently had seen a quite well-dressed woman in a Lexus pull over to a curb, go through bags that had been left out for the scavenger service, and take some of them away with her.

I opened one of the bags and looked inside. Pillows and sheets. In another, shoes. In the blue bin, papers. I looked around. There was no one. Not even a passing car. My hand moved with a will of its own. I took a handful of papers and stuffed them in my daypack with the racquet and balls. Then,

I grabbed more. It was a greedy and strange moment. I filled the pack to capacity and went on my way. My clothes were wet, and the contents of my pack were damp by the time I reached home.

What treasure had I grasped during my moment of insanity? School work! There were blue books and various term papers, all bearing the same name: Katherine Marx. Had Mr. Marx, like me, had a child?

The papers were crumpled. Some were held together by rusted paper clips, and the entire mass smelled of mildew. I organized them by type—exam books, homework assignments, term papers, all with undergraduate course numbers—and then by date within their categories, spanning two academic years—English, Humanities, and Film. All graded A+ or A. One odd item had no grade and no course number. It was a short story titled "The Dead Do No Harm."

As a parent I had no experience of the kind that these papers signified. My son had not gone to college. He had not moved into a dormitory room, then to an apartment, then to another apartment, and so on, shedding unwanted possessions as he went, depositing some of them at home before moving on to the next chapter of young adult life. From him, I had no college papers or other college junk. For that matter, no school sports trophies, photos, old books, clothes, toys—nothing—and, of course, until now, I'd had no fixed home for storing such things. It was impossible to imagine having such things to store and complaining, as one of my old library colleagues used to do, about stuff that needed to be cleaned out. As I surveyed my hoard, I couldn't imagine ever parting with a scrap of anything that Gregor, glad to move on, had left behind for me to keep or not to keep.

As a young woman, I had been in love. The compulsion that suddenly overwhelmed me was a lot like love, or infatuation, but it was not love. Its object had been a stranger who was now dead. Yet, now there was someone new. Now it was the stranger's child that I needed to learn all about and know. How can I explain? Something carried me along. I needed to know her, to learn all that I could about her. This was a powerful appetite for knowing that would surely never be satisfied. Love, for me, had never been like this.

The rain had stopped. Our house was quiet. I thought of the deserted dead man's house with its For Sale sign on the sloping front lawn. I dressed, put on my parka and boots, and quietly let myself out through the front door. The street was deserted except for the bus idling at the corner. The driver was pulling away from the stop, but he opened the door when he saw me, and I climbed aboard. It was 1:30 AM.

I got off at 33rd Avenue and headed towards the house that drew me to it. There were the bins, just as before, and some debris bags—large black plastic ones—that had been brought to the curb after my earlier visit that day. From these I took more papers, all that I could carry in my pack. They were an assortment, some from each of the bags. But this was not enough. I climbed the cement steps and crossed the sodden lawn. Was anyone watching as I, a trespasser, prowled the deserted property? I stood in the mud of the flower bed bordering the front of the house and looked through the window into a dark living room. It was empty except for a ladder, drop cloths, cans of paint, and shadows.

What had I expected? Not this. In the deserted interior, I saw a life. Edward Marx had lived his successful life and educated his child despite having caused my husband's death, my son's horrific ordeal, my own solitary, rootless existence. His daughter had grown up in this comfortable home. She had gone to college. She had come home for vacations. Holiday lights had been strung in the shrubbery. This man had never paid for his crime. My eyes burned, and hot tears came.

Another empty room lay beyond, visible through double doors that stood open, the place of family meals served at a regular hour each night. Perhaps there had been other children, as well, and a wife. It started to rain. I found my way back to the path, down to the sidewalk. Would there be a bus? Now it was almost 2:30 AM. I stood in the rain at the corner of 30th and Geary. Should I walk home or wait at 33rd for a bus that might not come at such a late hour? I decided to head for home, and the bus passed me as I crossed 34th Avenue. I did not feel the rain and cold.

The house was dark when I let myself back in. Downstairs in my room, I took off my wet clothes and boots and emptied the sodden contents of my pack onto the bathroom floor. This was a much more varied selection of reading matter than my earlier visit had yielded. Glad indeed I was to have gone back a second time. Mr. Marx had been a conscientious keeper of household records, and what I now found in my possession were various contracts for work on the house by painters, plumbers, electricians, arborists. I read them. There were also instruction booklets for appliances and a packing slip for a laptop for which delivery the previous year in Venice, California had been unsuccessful. The recipient: Katherine Marx.

The morning gave me a saner perspective. The storm had passed, and in the bright sunlight, with the waves sounding at the foot of the bluff and a strong breeze blowing across the sparkling ocean, my nocturnal excursion and obsession with Edward Marx now appeared in the light of a temporary mental collapse, and mental collapse had never been part of my equipment. I'd had trouble and sorrow in my life, but I had pulled through. I had gotten by and done my best—always a good goal in tennis and life. Now, maybe, I was finally having the reaction that most people would have considered normal to have had years ago. I was not ill from the night's exposure to the elements and had not been mugged. But clearly, I had too much time on my hands.

What activities were out there? Surely, museum docenting, continuing education classes of all kinds, innumerable volunteer activities, including teaching tennis, and part-time work. On the hall table that morning were the day's *Chronicle* and the mail. Nothing for me, but I noticed *Biblioteca*, the librarians' journal to which one of my partners still subscribed. Did I miss my profession? Not very much, although I had always liked the supreme calm and sense of safety that it gave one, and, of course, it had been a rock for me throughout all my difficulties. I picked up the journal and leafed through the articles until I got to the classified ads. There among the listings, was one that immediately caught my attention.

A UCLA librarian needed a temporary replacement during a two-month leave. He lived in a guest cottage in Santa Monica Canyon, and it would be available to his temporary replacement as a sublet. His car would also be available for use in town. A 20-hour per week commitment would be acceptable. Breathtaking, I think looking back, the deception I practiced on myself.

I had never taken a vacation in my entire adult life, and a change of scene would certainly be beneficial, as would some part-time work. Los Angeles would have changed a lot since I had lived there with my parents, but I should still be able to find my way around. I would go to the Getty and the LA County Museum, take an architecture tour of Downtown, check up on our old house in Bel Air, and go to the beach—just a walk from where I would be staying. I explained all of this to my business partners who looked doubtful because I had just moved in and also, I had a health concern, as they put it.

But after all, I had been accustomed to move around from one house to another, and this LA project would be like taking a vacation with some pay. I saw other listings, some for part time openings here in town—one at City College and another in a Downtown law library. I intended to look into these, but that intention was short-lived.

There was something enjoyably normal about working on my CV. It was odd at my age to be going through the process of applying for work, but it also felt like getting a new and fresh start. There was the question of my health—the very reason for my early retirement—and getting a medical opinion about my plan might have been sensible. But on the whole, the part-time commitment seemed safe enough, and it would be like going home again. There was a formal application process that included a phone interview. They made an offer, and I accepted.

I traveled to LA on the Coast Starlight with one suitcase. The sublet was a small cottage on a larger property with a pool, about a half mile from the beach and a few blocks from an elementary school with tennis courts that the public could use on weekends. It was a beautiful, quiet spot, with landscaping carefully planned to create the lush effect of a jungle. The pool, when you came upon it, was deep blue and surrounded by and here and there overhung with flowering trees and plants.

I was unpacked in minutes and after a trip to the grocery store, was settled. The day was windy but warm, and the Santa Ana winds were old friends. I swam in the pool and started for the beach, the feeling growing on me that I had made a mistake buying into the San Francisco house.

Now I saw it: I should be here. All of the bad things that had happened had happened in the North. LA was my home, and I decided as I walked that I would come back for good. I would come back to live in the place where the beach was pleasant and welcoming—not cold with wild surf crashing on rocks—and where old ladies gardened in the nude by their pools, and you could shop at any hour at Ralph's. Why hadn't I seen it before?

One day, I drove to our old house on Stone Canyon Road and parked across the street. Whatever anxiety I'd had about its fate dissipated when I saw it. The place looked lovely—impeccably maintained, and more artfully landscaped even than in our day, with the sycamore's low-branching habit preserved.

My temporary job was comfortable and undemanding. I would try to find something more permanent and would see what was available in the way of long-term lodging. Getting out of my business arrangement might be complicated, but it would not be impossible. As the days passed, I explored other work leads and found interesting rentals—not that I could commit now, but at least there were attractive possibilities.

Then something happened that confirmed my decision. The librarian whose place I was filling phoned from Boston to let me know that he would not after all be coming back. Would I like to stay on? My answer was affirmative, although of course, I hadn't taken even the first step in extricating myself from my current financial involvement. But I would work all of it out.

An unexpected result of my new plan was that the more I mulled it over, the more I had to face the depth of the unhappiness I'd lived with and not admitted during the many years of my life in the North. Moving back to LA would be like shedding an old, dead skin. But what about the man who had not paid for his crime? What about Edward Marx with his profession, his large and comfortable home, and his daughter in her golden beach world, the privileged San Francisco existence traded for an airy beachfront cottage?

So I drove to Venice early one afternoon and strolled along Ocean Front Walk. I happened to remember the address on the delivery slip that I found in Mr. Marx's trash bag. On I walked until I saw it.

A gentrified cottage ensconced in Southern California beach glamour? No. The place was dirty and decrepit, an old one-story stucco building consisting of little apartments built around a bare, ugly courtyard. The building was an indiscriminate brown and badly stained. The paint on the wood window frames was gone. The doors had glass panes, some cracked, here and there a wood replacement. The windows at the front of the building were barred and surrounded by graffiti. Some of the apartments had rusted doorbells, some had holes where doorbells once had been. The second apartment from the front on the right had something white pasted on the inside of a glass pane and, incongruously, a powder blue two-dog coupler lead hanging from the doorknob. I walked over and read the name: MARX. The dog lead had an alligator design printed on it.

I found an empty bench at the edge of the beach and sat down, watching the surf, now and then glancing at the place where Edward Marx' daughter lived, and thinking. Coming to LA for the temporary job had turned out to be a good thing, but this trip to Venice to spy on a total stranger was just plain neurotic. I decided to sit for a while and enjoy the fresh breeze and the view of the white-capped ocean, go back to Santa Monica and enjoy life, and leave Venice alone. The sun warmed my face, and I closed my eyes, shutting out the few surfers in wetsuits bobbing on the sea, the dog walkers, and the two women passing out snacks to a group of young children. The smell of the beach and sound of the waves took me to a better, more wholesome place in my mind. A snorting sound brought me back to the present.

Beside me on the bench, a woman had appeared with two dogs on a coupler lead. It was powder blue with alligators on it. One, a golden retriever, sat grinning pleasantly at me. The other, a pug and the source of the snorting sounds, noisily slurped water from a bowl.

"Sorry about the noise," she said unapologetically, almost haughtily, indicating the Pug. "Alfred here needs to rest for a minute."

"Is he OK?"

"More or less. Ogden"—nodding towards the golden—"is a bit younger. Alfred has a heart problem."

"It's nice that he's still with you."

"He's not mine," she said. "I just walk these two."

The expensive and new looking leash was certainly at odds with her shabby outfit—faded jeans in need of washing and a pink knitted poncho over a sweatshirt. She was a rather stunning woman, with a beautiful Semitic face, dark hair so thick that the strong breeze scarcely moved it, and a look of considerable intelligence. But she also had pallid lips and an unhealthy yellowish look. The skin on her hands was cracked and irritated-looking. She might have been in her early forties, but it was hard to tell.

"My daily dog fix," she said to the air, not to me.

"Have they been together long?"

"They're rescues. Their owner has only had them for a couple of weeks—two old chaps with health issues."

She didn't seem the type for chatting, but I said, "There's a group in San Francisco that rescues older animals with health problems and adopts them out."

The woman beside me looked at me in an appraising way, making up her mind.

"I haven't been able to own a dog for years," I said. I closed my eyes again, and when I opened them a few minutes later the apparition had vanished.

I took off my shoes and socks and walked down to the water. It lapped around my feet, and I waded around until my feet began to be numb from the cold. As I walked back across the beach, I saw the woman again—this time without the dogs—and I stopped to look at her as she turned into the courtyard of her building. She unlocked the door of the second apartment from the front on the right, draped the leash over the knob, and went inside. I sat again on the bench and worked my wet feet into the sand.

For the rest of that week, I did my best not to think about the meeting Edward Marx' daughter. I went to work, borrowed books from the Library and read, swam in the pool, practiced tennis, and planned my permanent escape from the North. I did the math. I had accumulated savings over the years of house-sitting. And there were my retirement benefits. If I worked—even part-time—I could continue my payments into the 48th Avenue house for a time while still paying rent in LA and extricating myself from my business arrangement.

And all the while, in my suitcase was something that I had brought along with me from San Francisco, the short story snatched from Edward Marx's recycling bin. But I was starting over, and I should not have brought the story with me. Why go back and back, dwelling on the harm that was done, continually re-opening the old wound?

Good sense, though, did not keep me from reading "The Dead Do No Harm."

It was a strange little story about a young Chinese immigrant in the early days of San Francisco who had become separated from his mother and was searching for her. The pages were old and discolored. "Submission to the *Daily Californian*" was on the title page under the name B. K. Marx.

After that, I returned occasionally to Venice to sit with a book on the bench where I had first met Katherine Marx. Not every day, but often, to see—to watch—the child who, unlike my own, had lived to self-reliant, though apparently not thriving adulthood. I soon found that her dog-walking habits were unvarying. She appeared at 2:15 walking north, returned with the dogs and sat beside me on the bench—whether or not other benches were vacant—gave the dogs their water, headed north again, reappeared without the dogs at 2:55, and went into her apartment on Ocean Front Walk. She did not speak to me, and her manner did not encourage overtures.

At last, one cool, windy day, Ogden and Alfred appeared wearing sweaters. "Cute outfits," I said.

There was a very long silence. Then she said, "They also have costumes. A tutu—for Ogden—and Alfred gets to be Superman."

"When do they…"

"Halloween. There's a charity parade along here. They also have Carmen Miranda headgear and matching dresses."

"They're males, aren't they?"

"They don't mind."

"I would love to have a dog," I said.

"Why don't you?"

"Well, you see, I haven't had an actual home for a long time."

Her gaze took in my clothes.

"I haven't had a *permanent* home in years. I made a sort of career of house-sitting, which ruled out having a dog."

This appeared to be more information than she wanted. She poured the remaining water out of the dogs' bowl, shook the bowl, and put it back in her bag. As she stood up, though, she said, "Feel free to make friends with Ogden and Alfred. They don't get a lot of attention at home," and she walked away.

With the help of a bag of organic, 100% natural salmon-flavored dog treats, I did make friends with Alfred and Ogden, and to be honest, I began to be fond of them. I had told the truth about not being able to have pets. In fact, another possibility was opening before me. I could correct this deficit.

On one unusually cold early February day, under a cloud-heavy sky that had turned the sea gray, she appeared as usual with Ogden and Alfred in their sweaters. I gave each dog his treat.

"If you aren't house-sitting, why don't you adopt a dog?"

I was taken aback by this unexpected overture.

"Are you still house-sitting?" The tone of this question was slightly accusing.

"No," I said. "And I've been thinking about this. It looks as though I'll be staying on in LA. I could have a dog now, I think."

Her face relaxed briefly into a small smile, at the ocean, not at me. "You can find just about any kind. On the Web. There are rescue groups. You can do a search."

After several weeks of silence, this volubility was something of a surprise.

Exploiting the opportunity, I asked, "*You* don't have a dog. How come?"

She only shrugged, emptied the dogs' water bowl onto the sand, put the bowl in her bag, and left.

I paid my next visit armed with several print-outs from dog rescue websites. When Katherine seated herself on the bench, I handed them to her. She examined them without a change of expression.

"Which one?"

I pointed to a small check mark in the margin of one of the sheets beside the photo of a small, brown terrier/Chihuahua mix named Basil.

"You are not looking for a quiet sort of animal, then."

"He's the one I like."

I never saw a more sudden change in a human face. I had said the right thing. She smiled at me, a radiant and beautiful smile.

"Your landlord doesn't allow pets?" A bit presumptuous, yes, but the rebuff that I expected did not come.

"That's right," she said, seeming to regard me with a new interest. "Not without a rather large cleaning deposit, and I'm not working much right now."

"You've been ill?"

Her face darkened, and she was gone before she poured the dogs' water onto the sand and walked away.

An unalloyed benefit of all of this, however, was that I did adopt Basil, and he became my great friend. This was—predictably, I suppose—the kind of relationship that had been missing throughout my entire adult life. He was an older dog, and like me, he had a heart condition which was the reason for which I was not to have him for long. Despite his terrier/Chihuahua heritage, he was mellow and quiet. I began taking him to the beach with me for geriatric play dates with Ogden and Alfred.

One unusually beautiful afternoon after a rainy spell, Katherine Marx sat in her usual spot, while Ogden, Alfred, and Basil, reclined on the sand. All at once, a Jack Russell appeared, a frenzied animal barking shrilly and dancing about, trying to entice the three old timers to play or maybe just showing off. A deeply tanned elderly man wearing only a bikini swimsuit and wet from a swim came running across the beach holding a leash. "Caspar! Caspar! He's friendly! Don't worry! Sorry, ladies."

"It's OK—we're all fine," I said, as Caspar sprang impressively, still barking, into the man's arms.

"Rhymes with Jasper," I said, prompted by Katherine Marx' Film Department essays, among other things.

My companion gave me a sidelong glance.

"In fact," I ran on, "I think *Rebecca* was the only Hitchcock movie—out of all the ones with great out-of-door scenes—that has a beach in it. Action taking place on a beach, that is, as distinct from in a seaside community." I continued. "Fort Point is not a beach. What about *To Catch a Thief* and *Jamaica Inn?* And *Young and Innocent?* Hmm. Well, *Rebecca* is the only *great* one with a beach scene."

"Yes," she said indifferently after a long silence. But this was the beginning of a kind of friendship—strange and troubled though she was and complicated as were my motives—growing out of two shared interests: animals and Alfred Hitchcock.

She had been ill indeed, as I learned. Emotional problems; difficulties maintaining a treatment regimen—keeping medications on hand and trying to cope with the dulling side effects that interfered with her work, and her work was more important than anything. She had lost touch with friends and family, except for one friend, a script agent's assistant who occasionally sent her books and story treatments for evaluation.

Now she was working on a project with the goal of turning it into something saleable. "A book?" I asked, but at that point, she did not seem to want to discuss her project. Given the immense amount of writing done on Hitchcock, the odds did not favor her being able to contribute something publishable. Of course, I kept this view to myself, though disturbing possibilities occasionally arose in my mind—only there.

Mostly, we talked about the dogs. She was also interested in my work long ago in production design. She had also worked in film, she told me, and had some success as an editor. I was sorry for her, seeing the way she lived now.

On one occasion, although I knew the answer, I asked her if she lived nearby. She nodded in the direction of the little apartment building.

"Right on the beach!"

"Affordable, too," she said with a bitter smile.

A fine drizzle began, and we got to our feet. As I was about to say good bye, Katherine said, "Care for a cup of tea?"

Her apartment was stuffy, and the air inside seemed damp. The windows and glass-paned door were completely covered by some kind of Indian bedspreads. No natural light came in. There was a Murphy bed, a solid looking but stained old oak office desk, a straight-backed wooden chair, a faded and sagging easy chair and couch, the smell of leaking gas.

Katherine went into the kitchen to make tea. "Sit anywhere," she said. I sat in the easy chair.

Tea was Lipton's decaf. Katherine sat at the desk. She watched me, studying, as I thought, my reaction to her dwelling, which, of course, I concealed.

"How is your project coming along?"

"Not too badly," she said with a glance at the stack of mailers and envelopes on the desk. "When I have time for it. I've got some actual paying work right now," she said nodding towards the desk. "A novel to read for the agency."

"That must be interesting."

"You wouldn't say that if you had to read the stuff. Most of them are terrible, but you have to read them all the way through anyway. *And* write a summary with comments. *And* the comments have to be polite. It might be better just to give up eating," she said, picking a manila envelope with Bass Joseph Agency in large print in the upper left corner and looking at it with aversion. "So far, eating has been a priority."

"Is that a typewriter?" I asked nodding towards a case in one corner of the room.

"Quaint, isn't it? I don't use it much."

"You're writing the book by *hand*?"

"It's not a book. It started as a book, but it's a game. An electronic game"

"Really—what kind?"

She was deciding, I thought, whether or not she could trust me. "It's called *Re-Make*."

I waited.

"It's an interactive game. It lets you re-make movies."

This was the very last thing I'd expected.

"Movie re-makes are usually bad, don't you think?"

"Usually...yes."

"But in this game, you can re-make any movie with a wide selection of actors, and you can vary the action."

There were three rolls of what I had thought at first were shelf paper. She picked up one of them and handed it to me. Unrolled, it was about three feet long and covered with a diagram of incredible intricacy laying out many, many paths from which actions and shots could be selected. It was a flow chart on which selections determined which alternate paths were to be followed, and these, in turn, led to different sets of actions, and so on. All of it was handwritten and hand-drawn.

"I started a book, you see, based on work that I did in college. But I haven't done any *serious* research in a long time, and as it turned out, I didn't go about it properly. I think that I just needed to work on something, so I just charged ahead without doing any preliminary checking to see what work was out there. When I got around to doing that, I had a nasty surprise. So much already had been written on Hitchcock. And then," she said, exultant, "I had *this* idea!"

I was dumbfounded. Speechless.

"This is the sample game," she said and handed me a second and much thicker roll—two full rolls taped neatly together, parallel flow charts laying out the original movie on the left and one showing the re-make on the right: two versions of *The Man Who Knew Too Much*. It was like unraveling the convolutions of a brain as I went deeper and deeper into this terra incognita with its many strings of choices—dialogue, action, camera shots including angles and lighting— each descended from each previous possible choice.

I was to spend many afternoons with Katherine, going over the hand-drawn charts and talking about *Re-Make* in the derelict beachfront studio apartment where she gave full scope to her hopeless obsession. In her game she saw a chance of deliverance from her broken life. She was ill, very ill.

"What I haven't figured out yet is how all of the paths should be modified based on the *initial* choice of actors. For advanced players, we might begin with a selection of directors. There's quite a range of possibilities..." She glanced resentfully at the stack of mailers on the desk.

I gave support and encouragement. But she would never sell her game. This was obvious to me. She was a recluse. She had, from all I could tell, just the one friend at the agency. She had no internet access—at least not at home—for marketing the thing. How was she to go about selling it? I listened, I smiled, and I asked questions. So sad, all of it.

At first I had only wanted to find and, yes, observe Edward Marx's daughter, for invading his world seemed a way of fighting back. But then, having met her, I began to like her. It was impossible not to like her. She was moody, but she also had a sense of humor, and she was very bright and good company.

Oddly, she didn't seem curious about me—how had I come to be there, why I sat on the same bench every time I visited the beach in Venice. She never asked me where I lived. Those matters seemed not to interest her. And for me, the relationship actually became enjoyable for its own sake. After all, I was coming to live in LA—coming home—and this creative, albeit unbalanced, person was another artistic LA eccentric, not unlike some of my uncle's friends.

But as Edward Marx receded gradually into the background, my adventure took an unexpected turn. Over time, as I visited Katherine and got to know and like her, I also found myself thinking more and more of Gregor. I began to have vivid memories of specific moments with him, like flashbacks. These were memories that the years had mercifully blurred, but now, I was living them again. Gregor became a presence with us in Katherine's cramped apartment or on the beach.

The afternoon of my next visit to Venice was very bright and cool with a strong wind blowing off of the ocean. Katherine opened the door and stepped back for me to walk in. Something was different. She actually looked happy— relaxed, and self-assured. She made tea, and I sat down to wait. She handed me my mug and sat at the desk with her own.

The stack of FedEx envelopes had grown. "More work," I said, nodding at them.

"I'll get to those." She smiled again, almost mischievous-ly. "You see, I haven't mentioned it, but last week—thanks, actually to your reaction when I told you about my game—I called my friend at the agency and told her about it. It was so lucky that you came along. I haven't had anyone to bounce it off of. But I bounced it off of you, and you liked it—the concept, anyway—and I began to think that it really might be something that I could sell—really, that it was not just a fantasy. So my friend came over and looked at it, and we went to a copying service, and they made copies of both scrolls, and she took them with her. Today, she called me and told me that she found a contact for me at Pegasus eGames, and he wanted me to call him."

"My goodness—that's great!" I was completely taken off guard. The congratulations were not feigned. I felt genuinely happy for her, but this was wrong. "And did you call him?"

"I did. I had to leave a voicemail, because he's away until next week."

That night I had a dream.

When Gregor was little, before the crash, he had a Superman t-shirt, and it was his favorite. In the dream, I saw the shirt lying on the floor, but it was adult-size. We—Julian, Gregor, and I—were about to leave on a camping trip. But there was Gregor's favorite shirt lying on the floor, neglected. Somehow, even though I knew that Gregor would insist on taking his favorite shirt on the trip, I had not gotten around to washing it. How could I have forgot-ten? But this sudden disturbance in my mind was nothing compared with what happened next. Would I still have time to wash and dry the shirt? I bent down to pick it up, but as I was about to touch the sleeve, suddenly the entire shirt moved. In an instant, it moved again. And then again, but quickly, as though snatched by an invisible hand. Then everything became clear: a louse crawled out of the neck. The shirt moved again. Gingerly, I lifted the hem. Inside, the shirt was black with lice. I tried to scream, but no sound came.

The dream was a message.

How could I have forgotten my son, Julian, and my life?

It was Saturday, but even if it had been a weekday, I would have stayed home from work. An idea had come to me that, if I had been in my normal state of mind would have been troubling. But now, I was awed by it. It was perfect. I pulled my suitcase out from under the bed and opened it. "The Dead Do No Harm" lay harmless and inert at the bottom, almost forgotten.

Now, this story had untapped potential, and with a few modifications, I would make it my own. But how to begin? My time at the Bancroft came to my aid, and the landscape—the old Outside Lands of San Francisco—came into focus. The story's original author gave only a general sense of the uninhabited spaces. I brought in the vast dunes that were the area's landscape before it became part of San Francisco. I also included the cemeteries that once were there. Interestingly, the location of the asylum in the original version had unintentional irony—unintentional, I thought, because it was unlikely that the original author—and my intended audience of one—had known about the old City Cemetery at Land's End, where Chinese and other non-white dead once lay, and some still do. One or two other changes rounded things out. Dating the action would make the story seem like a true account. And authentic, since opium dens weren't illegal in San Francisco until 1878.

And the wolves? Another private joke—wrong in English, correct in Portuguese! But most satisfying was my new ending. How well it reflected those inner promptings that I only recently had come to know, the Little Fellow transformed into a monster. Then I added the enhancement of alternating footers pointing the way—not too obviously, I hoped—to an external source that would enlarge and enrich the new meaning of the tale.

This all had been fun, and best of all, I was being honest with myself and coming into my own at last.

Once my changes were in place, it was hard to stop. I began a new creative exercise: my own *Re-Make* flow chart! Casting was a challenge. I knew nothing of Chinese actors or films. But there was the internet, and with its usual open-handed generosity, it gave me enough information for casting both the original story, "The Dead Do No Harm" and the re-make, which I decided to call "The Hatchet Man." To the best of my ability, I reproduced Katherine's schematic design. This activity, though extremely time-consuming, was thoroughly rewarding, even though—as I decided—I would not be sharing it for the present, for it might point to me as the sender and lead to undesirable complications. My *Re-Make* flow chart would be just for me.

But then, memory served up another creative possibility. I remembered Julian's wallet and the newspaper clippings. Those clippings could be slipped in among the pages of "The Hatchet Man." But I had to think for a moment: should they be secured with a clip or left loose? Loose seemed best to give a sense of randomness, or accident, and add to the effect of dark mystery that I hoped to create. The small risk that the enclosures might be lost or go unnoticed was acceptable.

The day passed. I hadn't realized it was night until I walked outside on my way to the market. I bought a pack of manila envelopes. "The Hatchet Man" went into one of them, as did Julian's mementos. I addressed the package to Katherine Marx and wrote the name and address of the Bass Joseph Agency in the sender lines. There was no cover letter.

I put stamps on the envelope—probably more than needed, but I was taking no chances. I walked to the mailbox, opened the slot, slid "The Hatchet Man" inside, and almost immediately was overtaken by deep, flu-like fatigue. I went straight home, got onto my bed, and fell asleep. I woke a few hours later, took a shower, and slept soundly through the rest of the night.

At dawn, I heard the noises of birds in the jacaranda outside my bedroom window. There is no morning-after pill for what I had done. But if there had been such a thing, I would not have taken it, for what I had done was right and necessary—a perfectly designed act of personal retribution. I had transcended years of suffocating self-repression. It was like winning at tennis for the very first time against a tough opponent who always had beaten one on the courts.

In the afternoon, I went to Venice. It was a sunny, blustery Sunday; the ocean was choppy and white-capped. We had tea, this time accompanied by Japanese rice crackers. This was the only time Katherine's hospitality extended to any refreshments other than tea, and her demeanor and conversation were, for her, positively sparkling. She planned to phone the game company executive tomorrow, Monday, she told me, looking up at the peeling ceiling, already saying goodbye.

Tuesday, at the usual time, I went back to Venice. But Katherine did not appear on the beach, and when I knocked at her apartment, there was no answer. Back I went the next day, and this time, I saw something strange. A man came out of Katherine's apartment. I had not seen him before. He wore a long, filthy-looking coat and under it, a sweatshirt with the hood up. As he walked past where I sat, I could see his angry, wasted face and the dark shadows around his eyes that gave them a sunken look.

At 2:15, Katherine, Ogden, and Alfred were nowhere to be seen. I waited. At 3:00, I went to Katherine's door and knocked. The purple bedspread moved, and Katherine looked out at me through the glass. Then she opened the door. This time, I saw yet another new face. This was not the collected, reserved, somewhat haughty face that I had first met on the beach, nor was it the exultant face that met me on my recent visits. This was a tense, drawn face, and it barely acknowledged me as Katherine stepped back to let me enter. It looked as though "The Hatchet Man" had hit the target.

Inside, the air was full of the rancid smell of the habitual smoker, something I had never before met in Katherine's apartment. And the tea-making took an unusually long time. I heard a lot of movement in the kitchen, mostly opening and closing drawers, taking things out of them and putting them back. Finally, the tea arrived. I asked how she was and if she was alright. Yes, she was fine. Well, I asked, how did it go with the e-game executive. Not well, judging from the change that had come over her. Nothing to report, she said; he was still away. She was not looking at me. We drank tea in silence. Who was the man I saw leaving awhile ago? Oh, she said, that was Stuart. A friend? I asked. She did not answer. There was more silence. Katherine, is this a bad time? I asked, and offered to come back another day.

They had worked together in post-production and had been friends, she told me, at last. She didn't see much of him now, but he had come by that day, and she had the scrolls open at the time, so she told him about the game.

A game? What was she thinking? Another instrument of government mind-control. Video games destroy brain cells. Didn't she know that? Would it be played on the internet? Even worse, didn't she see? The internet was the most sinister, most pernicious invention of all time. It caused degenerative disorders. Already government and corporations were working to control the human mind, and the internet was their tool.

"You believed him?"

She shook her head. But I could see that the diatribe had been toxic. Just being in the same room with him would have depressed anyone, and I had not forgotten the injury that a self-righteous, emotionally shriveled man could inflict.

The pile of envelopes on the desk had grown. "Looks as though you've got more work from the agency."

"Yes," she said dully. "I haven't looked at any of it yet."

Not even "The Hatchet Man." So the change in Katherine's mood was entirely brought on by the conversation with her friend!

"Have you been out with the guys?" This was our term for Ogden and Alfred.

"No," was all she said.

The next day, again, Katherine did not appear on the beach. She let me into the apartment without a greeting, and when she closed the door, she stood looking at me for a long moment. Then, automaton-like, she went into the kitchen and made tea. Again the job took a long time, with much opening and closing of drawers and rattling of utensils. My cup looked as though it hadn't been washed since I'd last used it. Something else was odd: I did not see the *Re-Make* scrolls anywhere.

"Say, where are the scrolls?" I asked.

No answer.

"Katherine?"

"There," she said nodding apathetically in the direction of the desk.

"But where? I don't see them."

"In the jar."

For the first time, I noticed the Heinz 57 pickle jar on the desk. It held ashes.

"There's no point," she said.

The incredible, hand-drawn work of what must have been numberless hours, immolated. The exquisite tracery of pathways was ashes in a jar.

The stack of story treatment envelopes appeared not to have been touched since my last visit. It looked as though "The Hatchet Man" had failed in its purpose. Someone else had punished my victim.

Katherine got up, went into the bathroom, and closed the door. I waited, and when after some time she did not come out, I went to the door.

"Katherine?"

Barely audible came, "I'm OK. I just need to be in here for awhile."

"Shall I come back another time?"

After a long pause, "OK," she said indifferently.

That was the last time I saw Katherine Marx, alive.

My dream of coming home for good to LA was not to be realized, but the debt owed by Mr. Edward Marx had been paid. I gave notice at the Library and to my landlord and went back North.

I was the person who had grown up cherished in a loving family of accomplished people and had yearned for a life in art. I had loved production design, and with my uncle's help, I could have gone easily and with joy down that road. Then,

I became a librarian, a diligent and orderly person who had been able to survive personal disaster. Now, once again, I was a designer, and I was proud of my work. Would Uncle Marcus have approved of it? Probably not. The distinction between art and life was always clear for him. My design was for *both*, and it ended in a death. Others contributed, true. But at least I have done my best. I have answered the call of a higher moral law.

As a young girl, I had a dream. I sat on the bank of a river. The water looked black. There was a lot of wind, too, yet the surface of the water was smooth as glass. There was a cement bridge from whose shadow a rowboat with no oars slowly emerged. A cowled figure sat in it. As the boat cleared the bridge, the figure stood and the cowl fell back exposing a mass of thick, tangled dark hair surrounding a shadowed face, neither male nor female, grinning without mirth. The figure gave no sign of noticing me as it glided past in disregard of the first rule of safety in small boats: never stand up. I had the dream several times throughout my life, during my time with Justin, and again soon after Julian died, and once recently.

Have you ever in a dream encountered someone you know, but who did not in any way resemble his or her real-life self? Soon after I arrived back at 48th Avenue, a new tenant moved into the house. This new woman—something about her—made me think of Katherine. I thought often of Katherine.

Yes, I visited Katherine one last time, after the end.

"Who are those people, Ann? Your family?" She had seen the photos, the ones I brought back from Venice. Mimi had been in my closet. Why? There was no reason for Mimi to go into my closet. She must have looked closely at the faces and thought one of them looked a little like the new woman—Bella something-or-other. And what if it did?

I had nothing to be afraid of. Katherine had committed suicide. I was not responsible—not solely responsible. What I intended was not what happened, not entirely. It certainly was not murder. Besides, no one here knows anything about Katherine or her death.

No, there was no reason to panic. But I did. The mustard was a sudden idea. I was almost a murderer that time—almost, again.

Grays, greens, blues, trees, waves, gulls, horizon, ocean, sky: my set.

I have no family and no friends. Who will remember me? Only this.

--G.N.K.

Chapter 29

Wrong.

I would remember her.

I took my coat from the closet, buttoned up, and went out to walk.

I crossed El Camino del Mar and walked south on 26th Avenue.

The whole adventure had been like an illness, and the people involved—my cousin, Stuart, Ann, the other inhabitants at 48th Avenue, the police, Roger—all of them at times seemed to have been imagined during the delirium of that illness. Or else, at other times, they were with me, demanding notice, their presence powerful and determined. The journey that had absorbed me and brought all of us together in a confluence of errors had been like river rapids into which I had plunged and at the edge of which I now sat, removed from danger, but dripping, cold, and shaken, although given the choice, I would go in again.

The temperature with wind chill was in the forties. The corner apartment building that housed Java Mary faced south and protected the few tables in front of the café from the full force of the chilling north-west winds. With my coat buttoned up, muffler, and wool socks, and the codeine starting to take effect, I was not uncomfortable. I sat down in the sun with a latté—decaf, doctor's orders. The coffee was intensely bitter, although this could have been an effect of the medication. I watched the cars go by on California Street. The pale, leafless branches of the plane trees shook in the wind. Too bad no codeine could take away the aching inside.

Katy was dead. And if you wanted the key to her life, *Re-Make* was it: extravagantly imaginative and designed with exquisite and painstaking care, pathway by pathway, choice by choice, and then, destroyed—burned to ashes, yet saved in a jar—that fertile, driven mind once again turning on itself with lethal intent.

I had found G.N. Knapp.

Her memoir had carried me along, a sympathetic reader, until almost the end. Were the parts about Katy true? I thought so. Enough of it matched what I had found out on my own. It is an odd thing, but Grace/Ann's death left a void. I had liked her, until, at last, I learned what she was, a visitor from the mouth of Hell.

As for Roger, I would turn my back on his crime and on him. Informing on my father or keeping his secret: there was no good choice.

Could I recover the copies of the scrolls? Not again, came the warning.

At the next table, a man and woman in their late twenties sat down.

They were a stylish pair, he in a black cashmere overcoat, collar turned up, light grey shirt and darker grey tie barely visible; she in black Ferragamo loafers, slender black trousers, and a red coat whose narrow silhouette, like her carefully and assertively made-up face, accorded with current received wisdom about fashion. I listened to their talk and let its shallow babble wash soothingly over my numbed mind.

The young woman in red sipped her espresso and smiled winningly at her companion over the rim of the little cup. An intestinal virus was going around.

In a detached tone, the man was describing his stools. "The BMs were the same. Exactly. No diarrhea or anything, but weakness and aches and pains. And a headache for *three* days. This is the worst year for this type of virus. Everyone says."

"The one I had," the woman said, suddenly grave, "I could *not* shake it. It just hung on and on. And the diarrhea! *And* vomiting! Both!" She squeezed her eyes shut and gave a little shudder. "Then my mother—don't laugh—brought me over…Guess what?"

He shook his head and opened his eyes wide, then tilted his head in polite inquiry, although he had heard everything there was to hear, including this, whatever it was.

"Chicken soup! She *made* some and brought it over! God, can you believe it? And you know what? It worked!"

The man laughed—a whinnying sound punctuated by gasps.

"It's not funny!" she admonished. "Nothing else helped. Not the herbals, not the sweating, and definitely not Echinacea. The *chicken soup* cured my flu!"

Both were silent for a moment.

Then, the man said, "I had chicken soup yesterday. I'm still sick."

Neither spoke.

"Chicken soup with chanterelles. Nothing happened."

"Well, that was wrong. Chanterelles," she said disapprovingly. "It has to be the old-fashioned kind. Plain chicken soup."

"Jewish, you mean."

She nodded somewhat apologetically. She was Jewish; he was not.

"Where at?"

"What?"

"Where did you have that soup—with chanterelles, I mean?"

"Bizou."

"Oh?"

"Let's see. What else? Um…curried mussels—only that's not what *they* called them—a little salad with various organic lettuces—and persimmon tart with crème anglaise. And a St. Émilion, I forget the year."

"That sounds nice."

"Did I tell you about my brother? His start-up went public, and he retired at 29. So to celebrate, he flew to Paris for dinner and came right back after dessert. He took his own water along."

"That was smart. You can't trust water anymore."

"No."

"Like the ozone layer and the whole world situation. I don't watch the news anymore."

"Everybody hates us."

They sat for a while in silence. Then he said, shaking off the gloom, "So. What have you bought lately?"

                              I do glory yet
That I can call this act mine own. For my part,
The rack, the gallows, and the torturing wheel,
Shall be but sound sleeps to me: here is my rest;
I limned this night piece, and it was my best.
                    Webster, *The White Devil*. V.vi.

Author Note

K. M. Wood is a former lecturer in English at the University of California, Berkeley, where she received a doctorate in English specializing in the Renaissance and Shakespeare. *Death by Revelation* is Wood's first novel and explores the ties between loss, fear, and revenge.

A student for many years in the martial arts, Wood grew up in West Los Angeles and lives in San Francisco.